Praise for the historical fiction of Fred Bean:

Eden

"Well-paced, readable, vivid."
— Larry McMurtry, *New York Times*
  bestselling author of *Lonesome Dove*

Lorena

"This fast-paced historical novel set during the last bloody months of the Civil War is a well-crafted blend of action and romance. Bean's research is solid, and he is at his best recreating the horrors of war. The novel never loses balance or focus." — *Publishers Weekly*

"[Fred Bean] has taken a historical incident and caused you to relive it. . . . It's a great story."
— *The Sentinel* (Ft. Worth, TX)

Poncho and Black Ja...

"Fred Bean takes
American h
breathe. Bla
Patton, and
pages. Well c

... Cook,
...uthor of *The Snowblind Moon*

GHOST RIDERS

Fred Bean
with
J. M. Thompson

A SIGNET BOOK

SIGNET
Published by New American Library, a division of
Penguin Putnam Inc., 375 Hudson Street,
New York, New York 10014, U.S.A.
Penguin Books Ltd, 27 Wrights Lane,
London W8 5TZ, England
Penguin Books Australia Ltd, Ringwood,
Victoria, Australia
Penguin Books Canada Ltd, 10 Alcorn Avenue,
Toronto, Ontario, Canada M4V 3B2
Penguin Books (N.Z.) Ltd, 182–190 Wairau Road,
Auckland 10, New Zealand

Penguin Books Ltd, Registered Offices:
Harmondsworth, Middlesex, England

First published by Signet, an imprint of New American Library,
a division of Penguin Putnam Inc.

First Printing, September 2000
10 9 8 7 6 5 4 3 2 1

 REGISTERED TRADEMARK—MARCA REGISTRADA

Printed in the United States of America

PUBLISHER'S NOTE
This is a work of fiction. Names, characters, places, and incidents either are
the product of the author's imagination or are used fictitiously, and any
resemblance to actual persons, living or dead, business establishments,
events, or locales is entirely coincidental.

Chapter 1

Cold gray fog swirled around five men standing on the banks of the San Antonio River at dawn. The air was heavy with smells from the city across the river . . . the aroma of Mexican tortillas flavored with *manteca,* and *pan dulce* sweetbreads and *chorizo* sausages sizzling in cast iron skillets in kitchens on the far bank. A line of trees marking the river were still shrouded in thick morning mist.

The attire worn by these men gave local residents an explanation for their presence at this wooded spot beside the water's slow currents at sunrise, for all but one, a short, wiry man in baggy pants and blue sleeveless shirt, wore gentleman's tailored apparel. And their meeting place, known to locals as *lugar de muerte,* "a place of death," had been a long-standing site for the deadly duels that took place outside of San Antonio.

Jacques LeDieux, the man whose dress did not befit this somber occasion, opened a polished mahogany box and offered Dr. Alexandre Leo LeMat one of Don Miguel Benevidez's engraved dueling pistols.

Leo declined. "You know I prefer my own weapon." He reached inside his black coat to remove one of the most unique handguns ever to be awarded a United States patent: a LeMat nine-shot revolver with a center barrel designed for firing buckshot, an invention created by his uncle in New Orleans before the Civil War. His particular model was called a "Baby LeMat," due to its shortened barrel and lighter weight to accommodate his shoulder holster.

Jacques stared into Leo's face. "Is *un bon* day to kill a man, *oui*?"

Leo frowned. "It's never a good day when a man has to take another man's life."

"*Oui*, but it is far better than the alternative, *mon ami*," Jacques said.

Leo nodded absently, his mind drifting back to other times and places. He remembered duels fought on the banks of bayous outside New Orleans, surrounded by giant cypress trees shrouded with Spanish moss, as if they too had dressed in all their finery for these grim occasions. He wondered if something called honor was worth taking from a man all he had, or all he ever would be, for Leo held life too dear. He did his best to deal with rare insults or slights that came his way with the same good humor he used to deflect the much more common expressions of admiration for his paintings. He suffered from no lack of pride in his work. It was simply that acclaim ranked rather low in the order of things he considered important, despite private doubts that his art was, or ever would be, equal to George Catlin's, a master portraitist whose paintings made Leo feel humble, inept, embarrassed by his own awkward brush strokes.

Jacques turned to Don Miguel Benevidez's second and handed the box to him. "I hope your master considers his sister's virtue to be worth his life, monsieur," Jacques said.

Don Miguel's portly manservant questioned Jacques with a chilly stare. "Is the outcome so certain, Frenchman?" he asked.

Jacques's reply was accompanied by a twisted smile. "Twenty times Dr. LeMat has faced men in a duel, and not one drop of his blood has been spilled."

Don Miguel's face visibly paled in the growing light of the early spring dawn, even though the Spaniard stood a few feet away from their quiet conversation. "Twenty times?" the don whispered, sounding doubtful.

Jacques shrugged. "Perhaps a few more. Who counts these things?"

Don Miguel swallowed hard, running the tip of his tongue over dry lips. He regarded his opponent briefly, looking over Leo's black hat and coat, his stovepipe boots gleaming with polish and the odd pistol Leo had chosen for his dueling weapon.

Judge Bristol, Bexar County's registered duel master, cocked his own pistol and said, "You will each take your positions back-to-back, gentleman, and await my signal. Step forward on my count, turn and fire. I am quite sure you understand the consequences of violating the rules. I will be forced to arrest any man who turns before the count of ten and the sound of my pistol being fired in the air. He will be charged with murder. It is the code of honor among duelists and you agreed to its requirements in my chambers when Don Miguel made his application to settle your differences with pistols."

An eerie silence followed while the duelists stared at each other. Leo remained expressionless, wearing a practiced mask to hide his own fears. Would this be his final duel? Don Miguel appeared to have grown uneasy, fingering the lapels of his coat again and again. His eyes shifted back and forth, as if he were trying to think of some way to escape this deadly contest with his honor—and his skin—intact.

"Are you certain, Don Miguel, this is the course you wish to take?" Leo asked, seeing doubt in the wealthy Spaniard's face about continuing with the proceedings.

Don Miguel blinked as he stared at Leo. "Your violation of my sister's virtue leaves me no alternative, señor," he said, his voice sounding as if it were filtered through dust. "My honor leaves me no choice."

"A reasonable man will always choose life over death, Don Miguel. It goes beyond a question of honor."

"A man such as you knows nothing of honor," Don Miguel spat, as he seized one of his matched Colt dueling pistols from the box and abruptly turned his back.

Leo sighed, for the don had chosen pride over prejudice. As a physician trained to save lives, he found it ironic that he was again forced into a position to take a life with a gun, yet his own strict code of conduct would not allow him to ignore Don Miguel's challenge to settle their dispute in a duel.

"Gentlemen, take your positions," Judge Bristol intoned.

Leo turned his back, his pistol raised, muzzle aimed at brightening skies over the river.

"One . . . two," the duel master began.

As Judge Bristol counted, birds sang their morning duets, bullfrogs croaked to their mates, and misty tendrils of fog swirled over slow-moving river currents, a peaceful scene most would deem unsuitable for the death struggle about to take place.

At the count of ten, Judge Bristol's small-caliber pistol cracked. Leo wheeled and steadied his revolver.

Another shot rang out, echoing through trees along the riverbank, starting a covey of quail into sudden flight through deep forest shadows, quieting the throaty cries of the frogs.

Leo felt the hot rush of molten lead pass very close to his cheek. His heartbeat quickened and his stomach roiled. Perhaps the only fulfillment he experienced in a duel to the death was this momentary realization of mortality, of the effervescence and fragility and miracle of life. The few duelists he had known sometimes spoke of this same feeling, and more than one stated in words of his own choosing that it made him vow to live every moment of his life to the fullest. For the sake of a beautiful girl, a child named Angeline, Leo knew he had to survive this duel at all costs.

"And now, Don Miguel," Leo said, taking careful aim, "the advantage is mine."

Don Miguel took a deep breath and squared his shoulders, awaiting certain death with a show of courage his fear-rounded eyes did not reflect.

"However," Leo said, "as I told you before, a reasonable man will always choose life over death." He glanced up at the first slanted rays of sun, painting the horizon with broad brush strokes of crimson and yellow and orange, and inhaled the fragrance of wildflowers and morning dew.

He slowly lowered his LeMat, firing a thundering shot into the ground at his feet. As the echo of the gunshot faded, Leo added, "And I am a reasonable man."

Leo stepped back from the painting, nodded once in satisfaction, and added his signature with a flourish to the bottom of the canvas.

Jacques, at only five feet and three inches, stood on his tiptoes and peered over Leo's shoulder. "It's a perfect likeness of the mayor, Leo. Truly one of your best efforts."

"You believe I captured the depth of his ugliness?"

"Without a doubt, monsieur!" The Frenchman's hawklike face widened in a smile as he pulled off his weathered seaman's cap in a salute to the portrait, his thickly muscled arms showing a variety of tattoos where his sleeves were rolled up to his biceps. When he grinned, the long scar on his left cheek, acquired in a knife fight when he was a teenager living on the bayous of New Orleans, puckered and pulled the side of his mouth up, causing his expression to have a somewhat sinister appearance.

Leo wiped his hands on a cloth and turned to a row of paintings adorning the walls of their lavishly furnished suite atop the Saint Anthony Hotel. He stood before a portrait of an Indian chief and studied it a moment. "If only I could have a subject such as this sitting for me. George Catlin, my mentor, had the good sense not to waste his talents painting politicians for the pleasure of their overfed wives."

Leo recalled the awakening of his true passion during his years of study under Catlin at the University of Pennsylvania. He'd initially enrolled there to study medicine at the behest of his uncle François, but soon found he much preferred painting beautiful scenes with oils on canvas over carving disease and pestilence out of humans with a scalpel. Catlin, seeing some of Leo's early works, immediately recognized his ability and took him under his wing, adding technique and sophistication to the raw talent Leo demonstrated. He taught him how to see the world around him with an artist's critical eye, as well as the depth of a person's character, and how to incorporate this into his portraits so they were much more than a physical likeness of his subjects.

Jacques opened his gold pocket watch. "The mayor and his wife await the unveiling of his portrait in the hotel dining room downstairs." He returned the watch to a pocket of his gray wool trousers, stuffed into the tops of worn stovepipe boots. The watch rested near a noticeable bulge in his pantleg, made by the bone handle of a Bowie knife resting in its hidden sheath.

Leo scowled, resenting being forced from his recollections of happier days. "Must we?"

Jacques smiled. "I'm afraid so, monsieur. We leave in the morning for the wilds of Kansas Territory. The appointment today must be kept."

Leo brightened. "Ah yes. The famous Wild Bill Hickok of Abilene, a subject worthy of the years I spent with Catlin. Cover that monstrosity with a cloth," he said, pointing to the portrait he'd just signed, "and take it downstairs so the mayor of San Antonio and his plump wife can view it. Even though I've widened his piggish eyes and painted over the hint of arrogance in his expression, I doubt either of them will have the capacity to appreciate how kind my brush has been."

He turned to an unsigned portrait of a beautiful child, a girl with dark ringlets framing a smiling face. His eyes grew moist after Jacques left the room. "I do miss you so, Angeline," he whispered, overcome by a deep sense of longing.

He poured a generous glass of brandy, pushing aside lingering worries that it was a medication he prescribed for himself all too often.

Chapter 2

Six white-robed figures sat their horses in a red oak grove on a moonless night on the Kansas prairie west of Abilene. White hoods covered their faces. A bay gelding stamped a hoof, rattling its curb chain, ending several minutes of silence. In the dark these men were hidden from four weary cowboys riding night herd around a bedding ground, where more than four hundred Mexican longhorn steers, fresh from a drive up the Chisholm Trail, lay resting, chewing their cuds.

It was a common belief among experienced trail hands that Mexican longhorns never truly slept with their eyes closed, always on the lookout for any excuse to come lunging to their feet in a headlong stampede. Cowboys who drove Mexican steers up from Matamoros to Kansas would swear that not one animal in the herd slept a wink for three months over the thousand-mile journey. Trail-wise cowmen wouldn't argue the point if they had ever owned "Mexican-bred runners," steers that never seemed to tire of a spirited stampede under any conditions. This was the variety of longhorn being watched by the six heavily armed, white-clad riders from across the wooded prairie knoll, as a gentle westerly breeze swept across thin needlegrass blanketing hills and shallow depressions.

One hooded horseman spoke softly. "They're real Mexicos, all right. Look at them racks. Most have got at least six foot of horn spread. First gunshot an' they'll be headed in a thousand different directions at once."

"Just what we been lookin' for," another said. "If we can gather a hundred of 'em before daylight, we can make ourselves a good payday."

"Looks like easy pickin's from here," a third rider said. "Let's git it done. We're wastin' time just sittin' in these trees."

"Hold up a minute longer," a deep voice said from the edge of the oak grove. "Let's make damn sure no one else is headed this way. Talk in Abilene is that they're gonna make Hickok a county sheriff real soon, instead of a city marshal. I'd hate like hell to tangle with him tonight if they've already gone an' done it."

"I ain't scared of Hickok."

"If you ain't, you're a damn fool, Shorty. I've

seen that sumbitch shoot. He don't miss very often, an' he's quicker on the draw than any shootist in Abilene."

"All I ever seen him shoot was stray dogs. Hell, he's drunk most of the time, or off someplace with one of them painted-up saloon whores."

"He's a better shooter drunk than you are sober, so don't take Hickok too lightly. I sure as hell ain't lookin' to buy me no burial plot just yet. As to them whores, sure as hell wish I had one waitin' for me tonight after we git done with this here job."

"We're wastin' time," another voice said. "It's damn near midnight. Besides, it's hotter'n hell inside this bedsheet an' pillowcase."

"It ain't no bedsheet. Better not ever let the boss hear you say that. He's real serious 'bout this Knights of the Golden Circle stuff."

"I'm real serious about gettin' this herd scattered so we can round up as many as we can. I need to make some money. We can kill them four cowboys easy, an' then clear out. All this shit about gold circles an' dressin' up in these stupid outfits don't interest me. Can't hardly see through these holes if a wind blows this hood crooked on my head. This goddamn pillowcase could get a man killed deader'n pig shit, if his horse is runnin' real hard."

"It ain't a pillowcase, Shorty," someone else

said. "It's made outa real silk. Now shut the hell up an' let's get ready to ride. I been listenin' to you bitch about that hood all the way from the shack. The man who's payin' us says we gotta wear 'em, so shut up an' put your mind on rustlin' cattle. I'd wear a pink corset an' high-button shoes if the pay was right, an' so would you."

Shorty bowed his head a moment, examining the robe he was wearing. "I've done some real dumb things in my lifetime, but dressin' up in a woman's bedclothes with a silk sack over my head, just so's I can steal some cows, has gotta be the dumbest stunt I ever pulled. Hell, them steers ain't gonna care what I look like, an' them night riders is gonna be dead, so what the hell are we doin' ridin' all over Kansas with these things on? My goddamn horse was so scared of me when he seen me comin' out of the shack he damn near throw'd me off. Can't say as I blame him all that much, neither. A cow horse ain't supposed to carry no fool dressed up like a ghost. Damn near any good horse would be spooked by this outfit."

A rider chuckled. "That's what they call us in Abilene, boys. Ghost Riders. Annabelle over at the Drover's Inn told me."

"I seen it in the newspaper," another remarked.

"You're a lyin' bastard, Clyde. Every man in this bunch knows you can't read a damn word.

You're plumb ignorant, so don't be claimin' you can read no newspaper. You never been inside a schoolhouse in your life."

"Shut up, boys," the same deep voice said. "Pull iron an' let's go after them beeves."

All six horsemen drew six-shooters from holsters hidden underneath white robes. Shorty jerked his Winchester .44 rifle and jacked a load into the firing chamber. The rider named Clyde pulled a short shotgun from a boot tied to the pommel of his saddle, cocking both hammers, then resting the butt plate upon his knee.

"Soon as we clear these trees," their leader said, "spread out and put a night rider in your sights. Don't worry if one or two gets away. They'll spread word all over Abilene that it was the Ghost Riders who stole their herd. The boss likes it when he hears us called that. Just in case you've been wonderin', he's got another train for us to rob next week. It's supposed to have a big army payroll on it . . . maybe ten thousand dollars, he said."

"I hope we ain't gotta wear these stupid outfits again when we rob that train," Shorty muttered, edging his horse over to the last of the oak trees. "Passengers see us all fancied-up like this, they're liable to bust a rib laughin'."

"Shut up, Shorty," Clyde said as he spurred his horse out of the grove.

*   *   *

Casper Weeks saw a sight that abruptly ended the off-key song he was singing, "Little Joe the Wrangler," intended to soothe away the fears of wild Mexican longhorns bedded for the night. A bunch of men wearing white hoods and cloaks came galloping toward the herd. Casper jerked his horse to a halt, standing up in his stirrups to make sure his eyes weren't playing tricks on him in the dark. "Son of a bitch!" he cried, turning in the saddle to shout a warning to Lucky Starnes and Bill Willingham. He pointed to a wooded hilltop north of the herd where he saw the white apparitions racing toward them. "It's them Ghost Riders a-comin'! I can see 'em real plain!"

The rumble of running horses' hooves brought the longhorn steers to their feet in an instant. Tails went up all over the herd and Casper knew exactly what that meant. A stampede was in the making, but of far more importance, he could be killed by this infamous band of cutthroat cattle thieves and train robbers.

His decision over what to do was easily reached. A thirty-dollar-a-month job wasn't worth dying for. According to accounts he had heard along the upper Chisholm, nine cowboys and railroad men had already lost their lives to these hooded desperados. Casper did not intend to become a number to be added to the growing list of the dead.

He wheeled his horse and drove his spurs into its ribs, bending low in the saddle while his sorrel broke into a hard run. Not a shot had been fired, but Elizabeth Weeks had not raised a fool for a son. Casper was getting the hell out of here before it was too late.

Longhorn steers thundered past him, scattering, snorting, and soon he was surrounded by stampeding cattle. Then he heard the first gunshot ring out, followed by a scream of pain from a voice that sounded like Bill Willingham's.

The rattle of cloven cow hooves soon drowned out other noises when four hundred Mexicanbred runners proved how they had earned their nickname. A brindle steer galloped past him with its tail in the air, bellowing, quickly leaving Casper's best night horse behind in a cloud of dust.

Casper glanced over his shoulder. Men in pale hooded costumes spread out over the prairie, guns popping in the distance, tiny flares of exploding gunpowder flashing from the muzzles of their weapons. Two riders were bearing down on him.

Casper was trapped by stampeding steers, with no choice but to travel in the same direction the cattle were running. If he tried to rein his horse any other way he could be trampled by a mass of flying, pointed hooves.

I ain't gonna make it, he thought, doing his best to spur his sorrel past a spotted steer in front of him.

A gun crackled off to his right. He saw Buddy Cobbs, an old friend from previous drives up the cow trails, throw his reins away and topple off his horse in front of a swirling, multicolored mass of bobbing horns and drumming steer hooves.

Casper closed his eyes briefly, certain that Buddy was dead from a gunshot wound, or trampled by runaway steers. They had shared many a night together, from South Texas across the treacherous Red River into Indian territory, to Kansas. For a few seconds he was flooded with old memories, until the reality of his situation brought him back to the present.

Casper carried his father's old Walker Colt, but like so many other trail hands, he wasn't much of a marksman. On the back of a running horse, jolted by the sorrel's rough gait, he felt he had no chance of shooting down any of the men behind him. His best prospects lay in getting away without any holes in his hide, rather than putting up a feeble attempt to fight. He asked his gelding for more speed, kicking his spurs into its ribs.

He caught a glimpse of Lucky, riding hell-for-leather out in front of the stampeding herd, leaning over his horse's neck while using his reins to whip the gelding's flanks.

Looks like Lucky's gonna make it, Casper thought, as the young cowboy's blue roan galloped up a grassy hill well in front of the herd.

But even in dim light from the stars, Casper saw it clearly when Lucky's luck ran out. His horse stumbled in a gopher hole and went down on its chest. Lucky went flying into the air as if he'd sprouted wings, arms windmilling, feet kicking, his hands clawing uselessly for purchase in thin air.

Lucky Starnes tumbled head-over-heels into the grass landing on his back as the longhorns thundered toward him. A living tidal wave of horns and beef and churning hooves descended upon him, engulfing him in its crushing roil. Casper knew Lucky was dead.

A break in the morass of stampeding steers gave Casper the very chance he'd hoped for. He reined his sorrel to the left and rode through an opening in the clusters of bawling beeves.

His horse labored for wind, its withers and flanks covered by foamy lather. Casper loved horses, but at this particular moment, with his life hanging in the balance, he gave the sorrel the razorlike tips of his spur rowels rather than compassion. He spurred the gelding as hard as he could, swinging away from the stampede.

Another quarter of a mile passed under the sorrel's flying feet before it gave out, slowing and panting for air. Casper risked a look behind him when he heard no more shooting.

Hooded shapes were circling the running steers, trying to force them to slow their run with a turn back in the direction from which they had come.

"I'm gonna make it after all," he whispered with the wind in his face, aiming his horse for Abilene.

Chapter 3

Bill Hickok sat at a table listening to T.C. Henry read from a newspaper. They were drinking wine inside the Drovers' Inn at two in the morning. Hickok was wearing his badge, and a brace of Colt pistols with the butts turned forward. Henry, chairman of the Dickinson County Protective Association, had been elected by a vast majority of residents and given a mandate to hire a new county sheriff who could enforce the anti-gun ordinance in Abilene and bring peace to the rest of the county. A former sheriff, Bear River Tom Smith, had recently been executed by a drunken visitor who chopped off his head with an axe. A man by the name of Roy Jones reluctantly took his place this past winter. He spent a great deal of time away from the county, fishing.

"Here's what the *Dickinson Herald* has to say, Bill," Henry said, after pushing his spectacles farther up his nose. " 'Hell is now in session in Abilene with the arrival of the first herds up from Texas. Murder, lust, highway robbery and whores run the city day and night. Seventeen souls snatched from this earth in less than a month, seventeen souls taken in their sins, ushered before their God without a moment's warning, and all this done at our county seat. Action must be taken, for we are fast becoming known as the meanest hole in the territory! We must rid ourselves of these ruffians. The council has passed ordinances prohibiting firearms, fining prostitution and requiring licenses for saloonkeeping and gambling, yet signs announcing the prohibition of firearms posted at the Abilene city limits have been shot full of holes by drunken cowboys. Let there be a hue and cry from decent citizens to bring law and order to Dickinson County, and to Abilene in particular.' "

Hickok took it all in stride, for he knew from whence his bread and butter came. "You don't really want me to enforce a policy of locking up these drovers, do you? Fining whores to put them out of business? Closing down gambling parlors and saloons without current licenses? Hell, hardly a drinking or gaming establishment in town would remain open. Word of this would spread down the cattle trails like a prairie fire, and the cowmen would turn their herds toward Dodge, or Newton. Cowboys three months on the trail expect pleasant diversions. If we do not provide them, you should expect to preside over a dwindling ghost town."

Henry sighed, nodding once before he put down his newspaper. "On the subject of ghosts, Bill . . . have you any ideas regarding who might be behind this band of cutthroats everyone is calling the Ghost Riders?"

"I'm a city marshal, T.C. No one wearing a white hood has shown himself in Abilene, as you know. These men appear to prey on victims and railroads in remote areas. If the Protective Association could afford to put fifty deputies in the field, it still would not be enough to patrol every mile of the Territory at all hours of the day and night."

"But who do you think is behind it?"

"I have no idea. Someone who is clever, and very careful where he pulls a robbery or rustles cattle. Their costumes may indicate some association with the Ku Klux Klan, or the Knights of the Golden Circle, although I rather doubt it. The Klan is not, on the surface, in the business of outlawry as far as I know. I know even less about the secret order of the Knights. It may be that someone *wants* us to believe there is an association with one of these organizations." Hickok smoothed his shoulder-length hair for a moment, thinking. "If I were appointed sheriff of Dickinson County, at a substantial raise in pay, I might be able to get to the bottom of it. But at present, my duties limit my authority to this township."

Henry looked askance. "There was the problem with Mike Williams, Bill. You accidentally shot one of our own policeman over that dog incident. Folks still remember it."

"It was dark, T.C., and I was surrounded by an angry mob of at least fifty men. Mike rushed up behind me, startling me, and I was too quick to pull the trigger. Mike was my friend. I am still saddened by what happened that night."

"I do understand, Bill, however there are some among the councilmen who believe you are a bit too trigger-happy. It may be difficult to get you that appointment."

Hickok's irritation was growing. "I'm asked to control a wide open town, where gunshots are the order of the day. But when I meet violence with violence, I am soundly criticized. A huge majority of local businessmen want things left as they are, for fear of losing the cattleman's trade. I see nothing wrong with an occasional shooting when a particularly rowdy cowboy is threatening the lives of others. Some of our troublemakers are professional gunmen and gamblers. I tolerate them, so long as they don't go too far. But as you know, I've killed a few and it serves as notice that there are limits."

"I know, Bill," Henry said. "You have your supporters as well as detractors. Personally, I think you've done an admirable job. As this newspaper says, hell is in session in Abilene this time of year. I promise to do whatever I can to get you that appointment to county sheriff."

"At a significant increase in pay, T.C. Last month I made more money shooting stray dogs for fifty cents apiece than I did from my city marshal's salary. The stray dog ordinance has seen me through the winter."

"You should enjoy a substantial increase in fines shortly, now that the herds are arriving."

"My small percentage of fine revenue is appreciated, but it puts me at odds with the businessmen I'm sworn to protect. If I lock up too many of their customers—" He was interrupted by a shout coming from a young cowboy rushing through the batwings.

"Marshal Hickok! A bunch of rustlers wearin' white sacks over their faces just struck our herd! They killed three of our night riders!"

Hickok turned in his chair as the freckle-faced cowhand ran up to his table. "Where did it happen, son?"

"West of town . . . maybe five or six miles,"

he gasped, out of breath. "I gotta wake up our ramrod an' give him the bad news."

Hickok gave T.C. Henry a glance. "It's out of my jurisdiction," he told the drover. "You'll have to find the county sheriff, Roy Jones. I'd imagine he's home in bed at this hour. Or he may have gone fishing."

"Yessir, Marshal Hickok. Can you tell me where he lives?"

Hickok shrugged, lifting his glass of wine. "Let me introduce you to Mr. T.C. Henry of the Dickinson County Protective Association. He'll be glad to give you directions to Sheriff Jones's house . . . but watch out for that dog of his. It's known to bite strangers on a regular basis. I almost shot the creature once myself, when it got off its chain. I would have earned fifty cents, had I chosen to do so."

The cowboy gave Hickok a strange look, even though the terror of his recent ordeal at the hands of the Ghost Riders still showed in his eyes. "You make fifty cents for shootin' dogs?"

"Loose dogs are in violation of a city ordinance. The same goes for that gun you're carrying. If I were to enforce all our city ordinances to the letter, I'm afraid I'd have to put you in jail right now."

"Are you gonna, Marshal?"

Hickok enjoyed T.C.'s obvious discomfort. "I

could be branded a crooked lawman if I made any exceptions."

"I didn't see no sign or nothin'. It was dark."

Hickok smiled. "Go wake up your ramrod. Mr. Henry will give you directions to the county sheriff's residence. The sheriff will look into this affair . . . but remember to watch out for that dog."

Chapter 4

Leo glanced up from his breakfast of eggs Benedict, croissants smothered in creamed butter and orange marmalade, and chickory-laced coffee. "Have you made arrangements for our private coach to be added to the train?" he asked.

"*Oui*, all is in readiness for our expedition to Abilene," Jacques replied. Since he was raised in abject poverty and had rarely set foot outside the city of New Orleans before meeting Leo, Jacques loved to travel and looked for almost any reason to convince Leo to undertake a journey to new places. The destination didn't matter nearly so much as the chance for Jacques to see country he'd never before seen. Though possessing little more than the most rudimentary education, Jacques was markedly intelligent, a fact not readily apparent from the roughness of his appearance, and he longed for new experiences as a starving man hungers for food.

Leo delighted in Jacques's appreciation of the fine books, music and art he exposed him to, and Jacques responded by allowing Leo a chance to view the same things through another's eyes, as though he was seeing them himself for the first time from a new, entirely different perspective. It was an ideal friendship in almost every respect, despite the vast differences in their cultural backgrounds.

Leo picked up a *Harper's* magazine to study a poorly rendered pencil sketch of James Butler Hickok on the cover.

"What a magnificent specimen," Leo observed as he examined the likeness. "However, this artist's lack of talent shows. I need to see Hickok's expressions myself. Several of them, if at all possible. He is indeed a worthy subject, but I've got to see his eyes, for they are the windows into a man's soul. As Catlin taught me, a true portraitist begins a painting with a rough outline of facial features, yet the proof of his art is revealed by the way he captures a subject's inner passions, almost always expressed in an individual's eyes, the lenses through which he views his world. A tintype of his face might help me prepare for the moment when he sits for me."

"Do you think the tales of his killings are true?" Jacques asked, as he locked the last of their trunks.

Leo stared at the sketch. The lawman's gaze appeared to be cold, glacial, as if he didn't give a damn whether someone lived or died. "If, as I told you, the eyes are windows into his thoughts, it would appear this man has no soul whatsoever," Leo replied. "I'd like to find a Daguerreotype of Hickok before we arrive in Abilene. I am, at this point, unwilling to trust the rendering of Hickok's expression commissioned by *Harper's*. I want a tintype of him, as recent as possible, to observe for myself what lies behind this emotionless face *Harper's* has shown the public."

"I have heard he is an accomplished pistoleer, that he has killed more than thirty men."

"While news stories are usually exaggerated, I suspect that in Hickok's case there may be more truth than boast about this penchant for killing."

"Kansas is a long way to travel to paint just one man."

"This is no ordinary man, and Bloody Kansas, as I've heard it called, is full of gunmen . . . the Earp brothers, Ben Thompson, and the boy killer, John Wesley Hardin, are reported to visit these upstart towns in Kansas Territory, according to the press."

"And you're asking me to leave the comforts of our hotel to travel to this den of thieves and murderers? Perhaps I should stay home and keep dust off the furniture, *non*? Kansas sounds like a terrible place to live. Or to die."

Leo grinned. He and Jacques became friends on the wharves and docks of New Orleans while both were children, and he knew for certain that Jacques feared nothing on earth, and little beyond it. Leo, born into considerable wealth, was irresistibly drawn to the riverfront area because of its terrible reputation and a young boy's natural tendency to go where his parents told him he should never go.

"A dwarfish Frenchman like you would surely be far too small a target for Western gunmen," Leo remarked, knowing Jacques was sensitive about his short stature. "Besides, I'd starve to death without your excellent cooking."

"Ah, so you admit you could not possibly survive without me?"

"I would survive," Leo replied, his face suddenly serious, "but life would not be as interesting, and not nearly so much fun."

"Perhaps an extra case of cartridges for your LeMat revolver would be worth packing?" Jacques suggested.

"I'm going to Kansas to paint Hickok, not to engage in any gunplay."

Jacques chuckled. "Monsieur, say what you will, but trouble, she seems to seek you out as surely as a Frenchman seeks beautiful women. I'll pack the extra bullets."

Leo inclined his head toward the picture of his daughter on a nearby wall. "Don't forget to pack dear Angeline's portrait to hang in our coach. I would feel lonely without her."

"Of course not, *mon ami.*"

The gentle sway of the Pullman and the clatter of iron wheels over uneven joints in hastily laid tracks would not deter Leo from his careful examination of a tintype of Hickok obtained from a friendly San Antonio newspaperman. The fierceness of Hickok's gaze was even more evident in the Daguerreotype than it had been in the magazine sketch.

Leo took out his drawing pad and began to make preliminary charcoal outlines of Hickok's features, while Jacques brewed coffee on a potbelly stove in the back of the car. He hoped he would be able to do justice to the character traits found in the gunman's countentance. Though Catlin told him repeatedly that he had an eye for minute detail, Leo was not quite so sure. To him, it seemed he always saw more than he was able to capture on canvas, which made him continually doubt his talent. However, three days of monotonous train travel from San Antonio to Fort Smith, then another day northwest into

Kansas Territory, left him little else to do with his idle time, thus he continued to search for the essence of Bill Hickok in his initial drawings.

"Monsieur," Jacques asked as he offered Leo his cup, "why are you so fascinated with these Western gunmen? Are they not simply murderers who strut about in cowboy hats, wearing guns tied to a cartridge belt?"

Leo put down his piece of charcoal to stare out the window at the late evening shadows. His artist's appreciation for beauty was momentarily distracted by the rich scarlet hues of red oaks and the brilliant greens of sugar maple trees, their leaves already in a full display of spring colors. After a moment of quiet contemplation, he spoke. "I fear it may be an inherited predisposition. When I was a child, my mother reluctantly admitted her kinship to several notorious Missouri pistolmen. She told me I have some of the Younger brothers' blood coursing through my veins."

"And what did your blue-blooded uncle, Dr. François LeMat, have to say about that?"

Leo shook his head, a wry expression on his face as he remembered his mother. "He never knew. My mother had a secret tendency toward violence which I fear was passed on to me."

He thought back to the way his mother's face would flush and her heart would beat so hard he could see it pulsing in her neck as she read to him from penny dreadfuls and dime novels, about pistoleers and shootists and saloon shoot-outs. It was almost as if she wished she were out West, involved in a rugged life on the frontier instead of living in a mansion, safe from the elements and lawless men on Rue Royale Road in New Orleans.

"Ah, this explains the two sides to your nature," Jacques observed. "I remember how surprised I was when a wealthy brat from Rue Royale showed up on the docks of New Orleans, and how fiercely you fought when the other kids made fun of your fancy clothes."

Leo hesitated a moment, unsure himself, whether his nature was due more to his mother's influence or her distant, violent relatives. "I also wonder about it, *mon ami*. The duality of my temperaments has always been a constant battle within me. I'm at a loss to explain it further. While painting is my passion, there are times when I look for danger. A dry mouth, the pounding of my pulse, and the moment when fate decides who will live or die. At times it frightens me, yet I can't resist putting myself in harm's way."

His eyes lost their faraway look. "A young Austrian physician, Dr. Sigmund Freud, has postulated that there can be two very different personalities inhabiting the same individual, often at odds with each other. Perhaps my darker side assumes control of me at these moments."

"Killing is not so complicated for a simple man such as I," Jacques said. "Some men deserve to die, and my blade is more than willing to oblige them."

Suddenly, the train lurched and began to slow.

"Why are we stopping?" Leo asked, returning to his sketching without looking up.

Jacques stepped to a window and lowered the glass, sticking his head out. The sky had begun to darken with the oncoming night, and the sweet scent of night-blooming sage drifted in on the evening air. "It is only another water stop, Leo. It seems our locomotive is always thirsty."

A hiss of steam and the scream of the brakes resounded from the coach's undercarriage while the train slowly ground to a shuddering halt.

As Leo added detail to Hickok's features, penciling in tiny radiating crow's feet around his eyes, the door at one end of their coach burst open. A hooded figure clad in a silky white robe swung into view, a shotgun cradled in his arms. He peered at them through a pair of eyeholes cut in his pointed hood, his gun aimed down the aisle.

"Howdy, gents, your valuables or your life!" The intruder's voice was coarse, demanding.

The charcoal fell from Leo's hand as he felt a familiar change come over him. His blood became like ice as his cheek muscles tightened. He turned an involuntary glance to Angeline's portrait beside a coach window, knowing what he was about to do, fearing it might cause him never to see her again.

Noticing the difference in Leo's expression, Jacques whispered, *"Mon Dieu!"*

"My hooded friend, why should we surrender our valuables to you?" Leo asked, his voice betraying none of the tension and fear he felt. Under his coat, his hands quivered like strings on a violin playing a concerto by Vivaldi and his fingers curled as he prepared to draw the gun holstered below his arm. Nervous sweat rolled from his armpits, trickling down his sides.

The robber hesitated. " 'Cause I'm the one holdin' the gun, you damn fool!"

Leo reached inside his coat with a calm belying his purpose, his hands now rock steady, as if to hand over his purse. Now that he was committed to act, the anxiety within him slipped away and his gaze went flat.

A pistol appeared quickly in Leo's fist and he fired once, the shell exploding with a deafening roar, filling the confines of the railroad car with a billowing cloud of gunsmoke and the acrid smell of cordite. White cloth puckered inward as a third hole opened in the outlaw's hood between the eye slits. The intruder staggered back, his arms flung wide, a crimson stain blossoming across the front of his shrouded head.

Jacques let out the breath he was holding as the bandit thudded to the floor, still clutching his shotgun, as if it might somehow save his life. *"Fils de putain* . . . son of a bitch!" Jacques spat, staring at the man's limp body.

Leo spoke softly, addressing the would-be thief. "It would seem you are not the only one with a gun on this train, *monsieur.* Were you able to speak, you might now regret aiming a shotgun at me and calling me a damn fool."

Pistol shots rang out near the front of the locomotive.

Jacques grabbed his well-used Greener 10-gauge express gun and moved rapidly toward the door where the wounded outlaw lay. The bandit's right foot began twitching with death throes.

"Obviously, our visitor was not alone," Leo observed as he fed another cartridge into his revolver.

"Oui, monsieur, and now it is my sweet *Ange's* turn to take a life," Jacques said, caressing his sawed-off shotgun as he leapt over the robber's body and disappeared outside.

Leo got to his feet and walked deliberately to the coach door, his pistol dangling at his side.

As he passed the outlaw's body, he bent down and seized the dead man by the front of his cloak and heaved him off the train before blood could further stain the expensive Oriental rugs covering the floor. Leo walked out the coach's door toward the sounds of gunfire. As he marched toward the engine, another hooded robber wheeled his horse away from the baggage car and galloped toward him, a rifle leveled in Leo's direction.

Leo raised his revolver, steadying his aim, though he knew the range was too great for his short-barreled LeMat. The rider was under no such disadvantage, and three slugs from a Henry Yellowboy rifle went singing by Leo's head, pockmarking the flinty ground somewhere behind him. Leo felt a familiar weakness in his knees and an empty feeling in his gut as death raced toward him, yet he steeled himself to face whatever fate had in store.

Suddenly, Jacques appeared between two railroad cars, placing himself directly in the line of fire. The shotgun he lovingly called "Angel" belched flame and smoke, making enough noise to raise the dead. The bandit was blasted out of his saddle as if he'd met a mighty gust of wind, the front of his white garment shredded by molten lead pellets.

From the front of the train near the cowcatcher, a pair of similarly hooded bandits reined their horses around and spurred away relentlessly, fleeing the scene of their failed robbery.

"It appears you have once again spared my family from the necessity of making my funeral arrangements," Leo said. On more than one occasion when they were children exploring the docks around the port of New Orleans, Jacques had saved Leo's life.

Jacques broke open the Greener and ejected a still-smoking shell. "Are we keeping a tally on such things, Leo?" he asked with a crooked grin as he reloaded the express gun.

Chapter 5

A few moments after the shooting, a conductor peeked out of the baggage car, beads of sweat clinging to his face. "Are they gone?" he stammered, looking up and down the tracks.

"Looks like the bastards ran out of nerve," Leo remarked as he returned his revolver to its shoulder holster. He bent over, seizing one robber's silken hood and jerking it from the outlaw's head. "Not a particularly remarkable face," he added, tossing the hood aside. "In fact, he could be called downright ugly. Only a mother could love this son of a bitch, and even that may be in doubt."

The conductor climbed down from the baggage car cautiously, looking both ways again before he addressed Leo. "I don't know who you are, mister, but this is the first time any of these so-called Ghost Riders have been killed during a holdup."

"Ghost Riders?" Leo asked, glancing at the pellet-torn body beside the tracks, noticing a vaguely familiar bit of embroidery on one side of the dead man's bloody cloak, a representation of a coiled snake sewn in green thread. "It seems these ghosts bleed and die like ordinary men."

"No matter who they are, they are unable to survive a ten-gauge reply from my *cher Ange*," Jacques added, planting a gentle kiss on the scarred walnut stock of his Greener.

The conductor gave them both a blank look, clearly unable to understand how these two passengers could take a robbery attempt so lightly. "They ain't really ghosts," he said. "They's called that 'cause of them white capes an' hoods they wear. They've held up the Kansas an' Pacific two times an' always got away with what was in the baggage car safe."

Leo turned impatiently toward his coach. He wanted to get out of his sweat-soaked shirt as soon as possible. "How soon until we resume our journey? I have an appointment with a Mr. Hickok in Abilene and I hope I won't be late."

"As soon as our boiler is filled," the trainman replied. "But what'll we do about these bodies?"

Jacques made a face as he walked behind Leo along the tracks. "Leave the *batards* where they fell. Even buzzards and coyotes have to eat in this godforsaken place."

The conductor shook his head, then he departed to assist with filling the locomotive's boiler.

As other passengers descended from the train, a hazel-eyed, auburn-haired beauty caught Leo's notice. He paused in front of her and tipped his hat, admiring her expensively tailored green velvet gown. "Pardon the delay, madame," he said. "However, I have been assured by the conductor we shall soon be on our way again."

She glanced at the bloody figure lying beside the tracks and quickly turned away, her cheeks paling as she brought a handkerchief to her lips. "Whatever happened here?" she asked, looking at Leo again. "I heard so many gunshots . . ."

"Just a short delay. Four men tried to rob this train. I have business in Abilene with a Mr. Bill Hickok, and I sincerely hope we'll be on our way again soon."

"You intend to meet with Wild Bill Hickok?"

"There can surely be only one gentleman branded with such an outlandish name," Leo told her.

"Although I would never refer to him as a gentleman, we have been introduced on several occasions."

"Are you going to Abilene?"

She blushed, averting her gaze as young ladies of refinement were taught to do when speaking with strangers. "I am indeed. Why do you ask?"

"Would you consider joining me in my private coach for the remainder of our journey? As I've never visited the city of Abilene, I would appreciate your company, and you can tell me about the town."

"I suppose there would be nothing improper about riding in your private car. We are only a few hours from Abilene . . ."

Leo grinned and took her arm to assist her up the steps. "My name is Dr. Alexandre Leo LeMat . . . Leo to my friends. And this is my companion, Jacques LeDieux."

"I'm Pauline Matlock," she replied, giving Jacques a smile.

As Pauline stepped into Leo's Pullman, she paused momentarily to examine the coach's furnishings. "It is beautiful," she said, admiring expensive furniture, walls paneled in knotty pine, polished until they had a gleaming luster. A dark red Oriental carpet covered the floor. A large settee was against one wall, with a mahogany table and two overstuffed Louis XIV chairs facing it. A silver coffee service was placed beside the sofa, and a crystal chandelier cast golden light over the interior of the car.

"I have never seen anything quite like this," Pauline said, examining every detail.

"Would you care for some coffee, or tea?" Leo asked.

"Yes, coffee would be very nice."

Leo gave Jacques a nod.

"Would madam prefer coffee, or chicory?" Jacques inquired, giving her a slight bow, as if mocking his role as servant to Leo's grand host.

"I've never tasted chicory, although I've read about it in magazines about New Orleans." Pauline settled onto the couch, taking some time to arrange her velvet gown so it wouldn't become wrinkled. Leo sat in a chair across from her so he could get a better view of her face.

The train jolted and began to move. The slowly accelerating chug of the engine and the hiss of steam could be heard up ahead as the string of cars gradually picked up speed.

Pauline inclined her head toward a portrait on the wall. "Who is that pretty young girl?" she inquired.

Leo smiled as he followed her gaze to the picture. "That is my daughter, Angeline."

"Then you are married?"

Leo's silence was necessary, a time to collect his thoughts. His voice became husky with remembered pain. "Unfortunately, no. My wife died during childbirth, of puerperal fever, better known as childbed fever." Jacques, heating the coffee in the rear of the coach, shot him worried glances. When Leo talked about his departed wife it distressed him, and Jacques was always careful to avoid the topic.

"I'm sorry," Pauline said quietly. "Does your daughter live with you?"

Leo shook his head. "She is currently attending a boarding school in New Orleans, where young girls are taught how to become young ladies of distinction. It was my uncle François's idea to prepare her for the graces required by New Orleans society."

"Are you gentlemen from Louisiana?" Pauline asked.

"Originally, many years ago, we both grew up there," Leo replied. "I left soon after my wife's death to attend medical school at the University of Pennsylvania," Leo added, remembering how he'd hoped to study ways to prevent others from going through the agony he had when his wife hadn't survived. It should have been the happiest occasion of their lives.

As Jacques poured Pauline coffee in a bone china cup, she noticed an easel in a corner of the coach. "Are you an artist as well as a physician, Dr. LeMat?"

"I paint portraits for a living as I no longer, as a rule, practice medicine."

"What made you decide to become a painter instead of a doctor?"

"While at the university, I met Mr. George Catlin, a well-known portraitist who specialized in painting Western Indians. When he discovered I had some small degree of talent, he took me under his wing and helped me refine my techniques."

Pauline took a tentative sip from her cup, then she smiled. "This chicory adds a . . . rather distinctive flavor."

"You may find it somewhat bitter at first, but once you get used to it, you will discover that regular coffee has lost its appeal," Leo said. "Perhaps a dash of amaretto would add sweetness?"

"No, thank you. It's fine just as it is."

Leo waved Jacques away when he offered him a cup of coffee, preferring to fortify himself with brandy.

Pauline turned to Jacques as he joined them, in the chair next to Leo. "And what do you do, Mr. LeDieux, besides make an excellent cup of chicory?"

Jacques smiled. "Most of my time is spent trying to keep Leo out of trouble, but I occasionally cook for us both, in my spare moments."

"Jacques is an excellent chef and he manages

our affairs so that I can concentrate on my painting. I would be utterly lost without him."

"How about you, Mademoiselle Pauline? Tell us about your reasons for being on this train," Jacques said, resting a booted foot on one knee as he drank chicory from a stained mug, eschewing the fine bone china.

"My father is a cattle buyer in Abilene. I'm returning home from a visit to my sister in Newton. She's just had a baby, a beautiful little girl."

"And how is it you know Mr. Hickok?" Leo asked.

"Almost all single women within a hundred miles are acquainted with Mr. Hickok. He fancies himself quite the ladies' man." She hesitated. "You told me you were traveling to Abilene to meet with Mr. Hickok. Have you come all this way to paint his portrait?"

"He has an interesting face," Leo replied, finding Pauline's face every bit as interesting as Hickok's, although in a far different way. He wondered if she might agree to a private sitting; however he decided not to ask now, not in front of Jacques. Though there had been no shortage of beautiful ladies in San Antonio, Leo was always eager to meet another. Just as the first taste of a fine vintage wine is the most piquant on the palate, so the initial meeting of a lovely woman is the most exciting.

Pauline smiled, bringing even more color to her cheeks. "It is generally agreed among the ladies of the county that he is an uncommonly handsome man."

Leo leaned forward in his chair. "It is not only his face that intrigues me. I'm drawn to the look behind his eyes. They are almost feral, in a way hard to define. It is as if the eyes of a wolf or some other wild creature have somehow been placed in the skull of a man."

"My," Pauline observed, fanning herself with her handkerchief, "you are very passionate about your work."

Jacques chuckled softly as he got up to refill their cups. Leo heard him mutter as he walked away, "Among other things, *ma 'tite fille*, among many other things."

Chapter 6

Two dust-covered men entered the sprawling ranch house by its back door, leaving their lathered horses hidden in the barn. A young black girl admitted them.

"The master be in his study," she said, pointing down a dark hallway while closing the door.

Spurs rattled down polished floorboards as the cowboys ambled to the doorway of a curtained room, illuminated by a single oil lamp atop a cluttered oak desk. A silver-haired figure looked up at the pair through bushy eyebrows, noting the brace of pistols belted to each man's waist.

"Why are you here?" the man demanded in a thin voice. "I've warned you never to come during the day."

"We got trouble," one man said, resting his palm on the butt of a holstered Colt .44. "A couple of sons of bitches was on the train who could damn sure shoot—a stumpy little guy with a big shotgun an' this tall feller wearin' real fancy clothes, like he was a banker or a drummer of some kind. They killed Shorty an' Jim Bob. The little bastard blew Shorty all to hell, an' Jim Bob was layin' in a heap beside one of the cars with blood all over his hood. We took off. Didn't git no money this time. Figured we needed to tell you right away."

Pale eyes beheld the gunmen for a time, shifting from one to the other. "Damn. Maybe the railroad's gone an' hired them some detectives. Pinkertons, most likely. If they look too closely at either body they'll find the insignia of the coiled serpent on their hoods. Our secret will be out if they recognize the sacred symbol for Knights of the Golden Circle, and that could lead them straight to me, if they backtrack me to Natchez."

The other cowboy spoke. "That little gent sure as hell didn't look like no railroad detective, Boss. He was wearin' this stupid-lookin' sailor's cap like the kind I seen one time down in Galveston. Had his sleeves rolled up on an ordinary cotton shirt, an' a scar on his face. Tough sumbitch, what little I seen of him before we lit out of there. Stepped right in front of Shorty an' just stood there, calm as could be whilst Shorty rode down on him, then he blowed him to hell.

Could be the other guy was a detective, but the little one was just plain ugly, wearin' ordinary clothes like he was a hide skinner or a teamster or somethin'."

A sigh emanated from the man behind the desk. "There was a big army payroll bound for Fort Larned aboard that train, according to my sources. You boys let it slip right through your fingers."

"Those two gents knew their way around a gun, Boss, an' they was comin' for us soon as they killed Jim Bob an' Shorty. We was holdin' guns on the train crew while Jim Bob went back to rob the passengers, an' then we heard this gunshot. Shorty was gonna bust into the baggage car to make 'em open the safe, only that's when the scar-faced little bastard blowed him plumb off his horse with the scattergun. Made the damnedest mess of Shorty you ever saw."

A heavy fist slammed on the desktop. "Whoever they are, I won't let them stop me from having my revenge! Those railroads and filthy rich cowmen will pay dearly for what they've done to me! They banded against me to run that rail line to Hays away from my land in order to fill their own pockets. I'll make 'em all pay . . ."

A silence passed.

"We're gonna have to hire us a few more good gunmen, Boss, if we aim to rob another train or hit another trail herd up from Texas. Ain't but the three of us now."

"Spread the word in the right circles, Clyde. I'm paying three hundred dollars a month for men who know what they're doing with firearms, and they get a share of the booty. Find me some hard men, and do it damn quick!"

"Yessir, only we got one problem. If Marshal Hickok hears about us offerin' gun money, he's liable to start askin' questions."

"I'm not worried about Hickok. He's an overblown drunk who gets paid to shoot stray dogs in Abilene when he isn't scouting for the army. He may be good with a gun when he's sober, but he isn't likely to interfere . . . he's too busy telling newsmen from back East how important he is, and he only has legal jurisdiction inside the township limits. Forget about Hickok and find me some men who can shoot and who aren't too particular about where their money comes from."

"But what about those two gents on the train? If they're detectives . . ."

"I'll make a few discrete inquiries when I'm in town. Now, get out of here before somebody sees you. I'll ride out to the line cabin tomorrow night to bring you whiskey and supplies. Now, git, and find me some guns for hire."

Clyde was the first to turn for the door. "You

might bring us one of them crib whores, Boss. It sure do git lonesome out there."

"Don't be a fool, Clyde! Our identity, and the location of the shack, must be kept secret. No one goes to the cabin unless they join us and take the oath of the Royal Order. Right now, these Kansas hicks are calling us Ghost Riders. I can't afford to have anyone trace me to the Knights. Let these ignorant cowboys keep thinking they're seeing ghosts."

Clyde and his partner started out of the study. Jim Bob an' Shorty sure as hell didn't look like no ghosts, bleedin' all over the ground like they done, Clyde remembered as they headed up the shadowy hallway.

Ben Thompson, owner of the Bull's Head Saloon, regarded Marshal Hickok while Hickok read a brief telegram delivered by a boy in knickers and a sackcloth shirt.

"Seems those boys wearin' pillowcases over their heads just tried to rob the Kansas & Pacific at a water stop north of Newton. A couple of passengers killed two holdup men an' the others rode off without a cent. This just came from the engineer."

It was midafternoon, and the saloon was empty. The room was dark and gloomy, and the smell of stale beer, whiskey, and pickled eggs hung on the air like an early morning fog. A bartender mopped the floors, preparing for the evening crowds. Thompson scowled. "I find it real unusual that passengers would take a chance like you say they done, shootin' at bandits. Ain't ordinary."

"It says right here that there were four bandits. One was plugged right between the eyes and the other was knocked out of the saddle with a shotgun." Hickok put the paper down and stared across the counter at Thompson. Damn, he wished he'd been there. It'd been a long time since he'd had any real excitement to speak of. That was part of the problem with being famous and having newspapermen and dime novelists writing about you all the time. It sure cut down on the number of men willing to go up against you. Hell, about all he had to do now was look mean and scowl, and the troublemakers threw up their hands. He hadn't had a chance to shoot anybody for nigh onto six months, since he killed his friend Mike Williams, an Abilene policeman, during a disturbance over a biting dog.

"I heard you used to favor a scattergun yourself, back in your wilder days, Ben."

Thompson grinned, exposing yellow, tobacco-stained teeth behind fleshy lips. "Yeah, once or twice when I had the shakes from too much bad whiskey. Don't have to be too accurate when you're packin' a short-barreled express."

"I've never used a scattergun at close range," Hickok said. "I prefer a pistol. It's cleaner. No mess."

Thompson poured himself another shot glass full of whiskey with a trembling hand, spilling some on the bar top. "You ever skinned and gutted a deer, Bill?"

"Sure. Plenty of times."

Thompson nodded, then upended the shot glass and emptied it in one long swallow. "Well, it kinda looks the same. That double-ought buckshot plumb skins a man and shreds the rest until the insides and outsides are all mixed together."

Hickok shuddered. It was too early in the morning for talk like this, and his head still hurt and his stomach felt queasy from the carousing he'd done the night before. "That's enough, Ben. You keep on like that and I'm liable to lose my appetite."

"That'll be the day," Thompson said, topping off Hickok's beer mug from a jug of wine he kept exclusively for the marshal.

Hickok pushed a stray lock of stringy hair away from his deeply etched face. "Makes a man wonder, don't it? The army hasn't been able to stop this bunch from robbing trains or stealing cattle from trail herds. Hell, Sheriff Jones can't even find a single track made by the sons of bitches. If the railroad would offer me enough money, I'd track them down."

It might be nice, Hickok thought, to be out on the trail again. Town life was making him soft, what with the women and booze every night, and nothing to keep him sharp, to keep an edge on his blade, as he liked to think of it. Tracking down those hombres might be just the thing to get him back into top shape, and get the cobwebs out of his attic.

"It'll be a long summer, Bill. Little extra money might come in handy next fall after the herds stop comin' in. I'm closin' the Bull's Head down for the winter an' headin' back to Texas for a spell. Too damn cold up here to suit me in winter. Wind don't never stop blowin' till spring."

"I'm staying on, I reckon," Hickok said, pushing thoughts of tracking down the so-called Ghost Riders to the back of his mind. "I've got no other place to go, unless General Crook wants me to scout for him up north again. Looks like I'll be shooting loose dogs and arresting a few drunks while the snow flies."

Something Hickok said made Thompson wrinkle his nose. "You brought it up, Bill, so I'll say what's on my mind. How come you keep pilin' dead dogs up behind *my* place? Can't you put 'em over at the Drover's so those rich bastards can smell the stink an' put up with the flies?"

"Mayor Watson said to put them in the alley behind the Bull's Head so he can get a count on payday. At four bits apiece, there are times when I make more money killing dogs than I do being marshal of this pissant town. You got a problem, talk to the mayor about it. Tossing 'em in back of your place damn sure wasn't my idea."

The saloon owner let it drop as Hickok emptied his mug of red wine, his second since noon. "You told me some fancy painter was comin' up to paint your picture real soon. Hell, Bill, seems like you're gettin' more famous every day."

Hickok grinned. "It's those damn newspapermen. They'll believe damn near anything I tell them now. I told this writer by the name of Stanley one time that I'd killed more'n a hundred men, and he wrote it down just like it was gospel. Sent me the article he wrote. He makes me sound like I'm bulletproof." In any recounting of his exploits, Hickok always left out a number of details, including the identities of the first seven people he shot up in Nebraska Territory. A father and his six sons, and not one of them had been armed. The youngest was fourteen.

"Somebody told me a man has to sit for several days to have your picture painted. Can't imagine you sittin' still that long, not with bad nerves like yours."

Hickok frowned, wondering what Thompson meant by that remark about bad nerves, then he decided to let it drop. It was too early in the day to get into an argument, and it would only make his headache worse. "Depends. I agreed to it after he wrote me a letter. Sent me his card. Downright unusual, his card was. I keep it over at the office. His name's LeMat, and on the card it says he's a painter, and that his gun is for hire. Mighty damn unusual, to be a painter and a hired gun. I agreed to it out of curiosity . . . just to see what he looks like."

"A shootist painter?" Thompson chuckled. "You can bet he's either a lousy shot or a real bad painter. The two don't ordinarily go together."

"It won't be long till I get a look at him," Hickok replied, pouring himself more wine. "He's due in Abilene sometime this month. If he can't paint worth a damn, I'll call him out and blow a hole through him, just for wasting my time."

Thompson pushed his heavy body out of the

chair. "I gotta shut that back door, Bill, so the stink from them dead dogs'll stop driftin' through here. Damn near enough to make me sick to my stomach."

He sauntered off to close a door leading to the alley as Hickok downed more imported French wine, hoping a little "hair of the dog" would stop the pounding in his head and ease the ache in his stomach.

Chapter 7

As soon as the train chugged into Abilene and ground to a slow, squealing halt, Jacques hurried into the station to make arrangements to have their private car uncoupled and moved to a sidetrack for the duration of their stay.

Leo took Pauline's arm and assisted her as she climbed down the coach steps. He touched the brim of his hat and gave her a small bow. "If you will excuse me, Mademoiselle Pauline, I will arrange for a carriage to transport us to town."

"Oh, there's no need for that, Dr. LeMat. The railroad provides a public surrey for that purpose."

Leo glanced at a dust-laden roofed wagon standing near the tracks, its unkempt driver leaning against a wheel while other passengers boarded by a set of rear steps. "I do not intend to allow you to ride into town in that contraption. Someone such as you deserves to drive into the city in comfort worthy of a lady."

He walked toward the depot, emerging a few minutes later with arrangements made for more suitable transportation. "It is done," he said, as a canopied black carriage with gleaming brass trim, pulled by a team of bay horses with braided tails and manes, appeared from the far side of the depot.

Pauline seemed embarrassed, obviously taken by the beauty of the surrey and Leo's gesture to hire it for her short drive to the city.

"Oh!" Pauline exclaimed, momentarily startled when Jacques appeared at her side. "Goodness, Mr. LeDieux, you frightened me. I didn't hear you walk up behind me."

"I am truly sorry, Mademoiselle Pauline," Jacques said.

"He cannot help it, Pauline," Leo said. "Since his youth on the back streets of New Orleans, stealth and soundless feet have been necessary for Jacques's survival. I fear moving quietly has become part of his nature."

Leo took her elbow and helped her up into the carriage, as Jacques entered the other side. The two men sat on either side of Pauline as the driver, wearing a dark coat and top hat, gave a tiny flick of a thin whip. The heavy draft horses began to move with ponderous grace toward Abilene.

"Is it a lengthy journey to the city proper?" Leo asked.

"About three miles," Pauline answered. "They had to build the train station this far from town because the cattle pens and feed lots are situated next to the tracks for easy unloading." She hesitated. "In the summer heat, the odor can become quite unpleasant."

The carriage took them down a dusty dirt road running between plank-built cattle pens that seemed to stretch for miles in either direction. Though it was an off season for the transportation of cattle by train, and most cattle herds would not be arriving for a few weeks, some of the corrals were already crowded with animals. The bawling of cows was constant and annoying, making conversation difficult. The crisp, morning air was redolent with the smell of fresh manure.

Pauline held her silk handkerchief up to her face, while Jacques did the same with a bandanna. Leo sat stoically in the carriage seat, taking in the sights, his mind on the woman and his first meeting with Hickok.

Away from the cattle yards, where breathing was easier, Leo spoke. "I did not see any ranches or livestock on the way into town. Are there no ranchers or farms in Kansas?"

Pauline smiled. "Of course there are, but most

are not near Abilene itself. The open plains in this area are not well suited for cattle grazing or farming. The town is used more as a destination for the huge cattle drives that come up from Texas and Mexico. The animals are driven here overland and held in feed lots until they fatten up. Then they are shipped to Chicago for slaughter."

"I see," Leo said. "And your father, you said he is a cattle buyer?"

She nodded. "Yes. He has arrangements with many of the larger ranchers in Texas and Mexico to sell him their beeves when they get them this far, then he sells the animals to rendering plants in Chicago."

Jacques stroked his chin, unconsciously fingering the scar on his left cheek. "It would seem to make more sense for the men in Chicago to deal directly with the ranchers, thus making more profits for themselves by eliminating the man in between."

Leo wagged his head. "I told you Jacques was a fine manager. He is always thinking of ways to squeeze another penny out of every dollar."

"Yes, Jacques, it would make the men in Chicago more money to do it that way, but then they would have to pay someone to be here when the cattle arrived, to pay the ranchers and to make sure the counts are correct and that there are no sick or poor quality animals being sold," Pauline said. "So you see, in the end, it is cheaper for them to let my father and others do that job."

They soon arrived at the outskirts of Abilene, a few buildings now coming into view. For the most part, they were wooden storefronts with large, canvas, tentlike structures behind them. It seemed to Leo as if every other structure was a saloon or gambling hall or whorehouse.

It looked to be a populous town. Buckboards, horses, and people on foot all coursed up and down the streets in both directions. There were children playing in the roadways, running in small groups back and forth, dodging piles of horse and dog manure, unmindful of the traffic surrounding them. Packs of dogs roamed freely, occasionally causing a horse to rear or a buckboard team to shy away, cursing drivers shouting epithets at the offending curs. Leo thought the smell of the town was not much of an improvement over that of the cattle pens.

The noise from all this activity was a constant drone of barking dogs, whinnying horses, shouting men, and screaming children.

"Why are so many buildings made of canvas?" Jacques asked Pauline.

"Wood is somewhat scarce out here on the plains. It has to be brought in by Studebaker wagons or on the train, making the cost prohibitive for many of the smaller businesses. However, as we get into the main part of town, you will see many fine houses and buildings. In fact, I would suggest you stay at the Drover's Inn. It is one of the finest for hundreds of miles."

"The Drover's Inn?"

"It's where ranchers and local cattle buyers meet to eat, drink, and make their deals for buying the herds. It's quite lively most of the time, however it is quiet late at night. And the food is excellent."

Pauline was right; the deeper into Abilene they drove, the finer and more elaborate most buildings and houses became, and there were far fewer saloons. They passed several banks along the way. Here, the streets were lined with boardwalks.

The Drover's Inn was in the center of town, situated on the main street, and it was just as Pauline described it, being among the better establishments Leo had seen.

The Drover's stood three stories high, a full story taller than surrounding buildings, built of whitewashed clapboard with split wood shingles covering the roof. There was a wide veranda surrounding the entire front of the hotel, with dozens of tables and chairs placed on it. Waitresses scurried about serving the men gathered there. Most of the diners were dressed in business suits with starched white shirts, silk vests in bright colors and bowler hats or derbies. Some of the patrons wore cowboy garb, men covered with trail dust, their Stetson hats showing signs of wear and weather.

Leo smiled. "What a glorious mix of two cultures. The money changers and bankers and lawyers, eating with lowly working men. I wonder what they have in common."

Pauline laughed at the way Leo put it. "Why, money and cattle of course," she said. "They may look unwashed, but those cattlemen sitting on the porch are often worth more money than the men in business attire."

She pointed a slender finger toward the east end of the veranda. "I should know, for there is my father now. He and my brother James are sitting alone, so their shipment of cattle must not have arrived."

Leo followed her gaze to two men sitting at a corner table. Pauline's father was a squat, barrel-chested man with a face reddened by whiskey and sun, muttonchop sideburns emerging from a fringe of hair surrounding a balding pate like a halo. He was wearing a dark blue suit over a white shirt and vest, with a gold watch chain stretched across his ample abdomen. His expression was one of boredom, as if he were blind to the excitement and fervor of activity on the streets. But Leo noticed his eyes were sharp, and he judged the man was a shrewd businessman who missed little of what went on around him.

Next to him was a young man who appeared to be a year or two older than Pauline, somewhere in his mid-twenties. He was dressed more like the cowboys Leo was accustomed to seeing in San Antonio. He wore a light red and black plaid shirt, covered with a brown leather vest and jeans tucked into knee-high black boots adorned with spurs. He was tipped back in his chair with his boots on the edge of the table, and Leo could see a pistol on his hip, his tied-down holster hanging low on his thigh. Evidently the boy fancied himself a gunman, for his holster was in an awkward position for one who did any real work on horseback. He had a petulant expression, sour, as if he had been forced to be here against his will. Either he was very bored, or something else was bothering him, Leo thought.

The driver pulled the carriage to a halt directly in front of the veranda, and Pauline waved her handkerchief, attracting her father's attention for the first time.

He nodded when he saw her, his expression softening, as if his most prized possession was returned to him at last.

Leo saw James watching with undisguised jealousy on his face before he grinned weakly and gave Pauline a wave.

Leo assisted her from the carriage and escorted her up the porch steps, then over to her father's table.

"Father," Pauline said, stepping back, "I'd like you to meet Dr. Alexander Leo LeMat, and his friend, Jacques LeDieux, of San Antonio, Texas."

"Howdy, Dr. LeMat," Pauline's father said, looking Leo up and down as if he disapproved of his appearance. "My name's John Matlock." He inclined his head, "And this here's my son, James."

The men shook hands. Leo took note of a cautious look on John Matlock's face.

"Would you gentlemen care to join us for a drink here on the porch?" John asked. "I know it's early for some folks to partake of distilled spirits."

"Certainly," Leo answered. "Mademoiselle Pauline has been kind enough on our journey from the depot to tell us about your town." He glanced up the street at the throng of wagons, horses and people. "It seems a most intriguing place."

James leaned his head to the side and spat

in the dirt. "Maybe to you," he said, "but not to me."

Pauline grabbed her brother by the arm and pulled him away from the table. "Oh, Jimmy, are you still trying to get Dad to let you go to Dodge City?"

James glared at her. "Yeah, that's where all the action is, not in this hick town!"

Pauline shook her head. "You wouldn't be saying that if you'd been on the train with me."

"What do you mean by that?"

"You know those Ghost Riders we've been reading about in the *Herald*? Four of them tried to rob our train at a water stop."

John overheard what she said. "What's this about Ghost Riders?" he asked.

"They attempted to rob the train, but Dr. LeMat and Jacques killed two of them and the others ran off with their tails tucked between their legs."

"We hadn't heard," John remarked, scowling. "Only a week or so back, they struck a small herd of longhorns up from Sweetwater and killed three cowboys. Sheriff Jones acts like he can't find nary a trace of the stolen beeves, or the rustlers."

James wore a smug look. "If I'd have been there, or on that train, I'd have killed 'em all."

Leo studied James for a moment. "Have you ever killed a man with a gun?"

"Not yet. One of these days real soon, I'm liable to."

"Ah, not yet," Leo said quietly. "To take a man's life is to take all that he has, all that he ever has been or ever will be. It is not something one does lightly."

John called their waitress over, silencing James with a stern look. "Tell Annabelle what you gents want."

"I would like a snifter of brandy, Napoleon or Martel if you have it," Leo replied.

"I'll have rye whiskey," Jacques added.

After James and John ordered whiskey, and Pauline ordered a glass of red wine, John leaned back in his chair and pulled a thick cigar from his vest pocket. After he got it lit, being careful to blow the smoke away from Pauline, he asked, "What is it you do for a living, Dr. LeMat? Are you a surgeon?"

Leo pulled a card from his pocket and handed it to Matlock.

John took a moment to put on reading glasses, then he looked at the card. He frowned when he read the card aloud.

"Dr. Alexandre Leo LeMat. Portraitist. Gun for Hire. That's a downright unusual combination. Which business is it that brings you to Abilene?"

As their drinks arrived, Leo explained, "I've come to paint Wild Bill Hickok's portrait."

John returned Leo's card. "Sorry, but I never was all that interested in what a man could do with a painter's brush, unless I needed some kind of sign painting done."

Leo noticed Pauline was giving him occasional sly glances, and he made himself a promise. At some point he would ask for her address, and inquire if she would care to join him for a carriage ride the following evening—with her father's permission, of course. Her unusual beauty stirred something within him and he fully intended to get to know her better . . . if she would allow it.

Chapter 8

Leo adjusted the drapes on a window to let more sunlight into their room on the top floor of the Drover's Inn. The morning was bright and clear, the air crisp and cool, a perfect early spring day. The wind at this elevation must have swept the town's odors away, for he could smell sage, hay and wildflowers on the breeze.

He leaned on the railing of their balcony and took a deep breath. They rarely enjoyed weather like this in San Antonio. It seemed Texas had only two seasons; a very short and relatively mild winter, then a long and brutal summer. This morning reminded Leo of his days at the University of Pennsylvania and the joy he felt when Catlin showed him how to mix his oils to capture the brilliant colors of all seasons . . . even the pale grays and blinding whites of a snowy northeast winter.

His reverie was interrupted when Jacques appeared behind him with their coffee. "Good morning, Leo."

"Good morning, Jacques. Did you sleep well?"

Leo had sent Jacques exploring the saloons of Abilene last night to see what he could find out about James Butler Hickok prior to their meeting, which he planned for today. Jacques had still not come home when Leo finally went to bed at two A.M.

"I slept well, but not for very long, *mon ami.*"

"And what did you find out about Hickok?"

"Monsieur Hickok, though apparently well liked by many, does not command undue respect in this town. Most of the men I talked to think he does a reasonable job as marshal, but it seems Hickok is extremely fond of red wine, in abundance. It's as though the men I questioned sometimes described two different people. Many claimed his appearance is slovenly, his demeanor rude and abrupt, and a few said there is some question about the truth of the exploits he recounts at almost every opportunity." Jacques chuckled. "While by others, he is described as handsome, charming, very brave and a man of great honor. It would seem he is also a gentleman who fancies, and is fancied by, a great many beautiful ladies."

Leo listened closely. This was an important

part of his preparations for any significant portrait, to find out all he could about the subjects he planned to paint. He felt a good portrait should show as much of the inner man as possible, as well as his face. In order to find out about a man's personality, you had to talk to people who knew him well.

"Are you saying that Marshal Hickok may turn out to be a fraud?"

Jacques hesitated, then he shook his head. "No, not at all. He's apparently done many of the things he's known for, and has on occasion shown tremendous bravery against tall odds. It's more that the episodes have been exaggerated, blown out of proportion by newspaper and magazine writers from back East who interview him.

"Speaking of that," Jacques said, "there's an interesting story of how he came to be called Wild Bill."

Leo gave Jacques a puzzled look. "Tell me," he said, for he had wondered about it himself.

"Years ago, Monsieur Hickok stopped for a drink at what is commonly called a roadhouse, a combination of saloon and general store. Inside were six or seven people, all members of the same family, according to the story I was told. The leader of the clan and Hickok exchanged angry words. When the man reached inside his coat, Hickok, thinking he was reaching for a pistol, drew his gun and shot the entire family to death in a murderous rage. Hence, the name Wild Bill. The owner of the roadhouse was unable to stop Hickok until the men were all dead. Hickok went on a wild killing spree."

"And was the first man reaching for a gun?" Leo asked.

Jacques wagged his head. "No. None of them were armed at all. One boy was carrying a skinning knife."

Leo pursed his lips before savoring the bite of chicory on his tongue. He considered what Jacques told him, trying to imagine the fear Hickok might have felt, finding himself alone in a room with seven possible adversaries and no one to back him up. It sounded like a mistake anyone could have made in this lawless country, where a gun was the only thing a man could depend upon. Leo sighed. "It's said that no man is a hero to his friends, and I don't think we can blame Hickok for the excesses of the Eastern writers. In regard to the West and its heroes, their motto would seem to be, when a legend sounds better than the facts, print the legend. It sells."

Jacques stood beside Leo on the balcony, sipping his coffee. "I suppose so. However, I'd hoped Hickok would be as impressive as what is written about him."

"Is any man?" Leo wondered.

"When are you to meet Hickok?" Jacques asked, noticing Leo had set up his easel near a window that opened to the north, in order to capture the best light for painting.

"I sent a boy to find him last evening, and invite him to dine with us at noon in the dining room of the hotel. Depending upon how our meeting proceeds, I'll make arrangements for the sitting."

At precisely a quarter to twelve, Leo dressed in his best coat and vest, arranging his shoulder holster so no bulge would show, and then proceeded downstairs to the hotel veranda to meet with Marshal Hickok. He had Jacques sit next to him, placing themselves so the noon sun would shine on Hickok's face, making details of his features easier to discern.

Leo ordered a snifter of brandy, while Jacques ordered beer, stating that he needed it to take the edge off a headache acquired the previous evening on his mission to the saloons.

Hickok arrived on time, and Leo harbored no doubts about the identity of the man who came riding up to the hotel on a dappled gray stud. Leo watched closely, paying attention to every detail of the marshal's movements. Hickok swung down lightly from the saddle with a graceful manner, with squarely set shoulders and no wasted motion, tied off his stud to a hitchrail and approached the veranda steps.

He was tall, about six feet and three inches, and weighed close to two hundred pounds. He walked with his back straight, his hands hanging loosely near the pair of reversed Colt Peacemakers at his waist. Hickok wore an odd combination of a buckskin shirt covered with Indian beadwork and faded denim pants. His stovepipe boots needed blacking.

Leo raised a hand, signaling for him to join them at their table. He noticed Hickok frown a bit, and the corners of his mouth turned down slightly after he gave Leo a rather cold, appraising glance.

"I'm Bill Hickok," he said as Leo and Jacques stood up to offer their hands. "Some of those damn Easterners have taken to calling me Wild Bill. I reckon you already know about that or you wouldn't be here."

"I am Leo LeMat. This is my companion, Jacques LeDieux," Leo said, feeling a callused palm when he shook with the marshal.

Hickok sat across from Leo and Jacques, ordering a glass of red wine from their youthful waitress. He gave the girl's body a close inspection before she left.

Hickok wore a loose bandanna around his throat. Blond hair tumbled to his shoulders, and his steel-gray eyes, set off by a drooping mustache, fit the image of the Wild West character Leo had expected.

At first glance, Leo found him every bit as forbidding as the pencil sketch in *Harper's*. But as they sat quietly for a moment, staring at each other, each taking the other's measure before speaking, Leo noticed subtle discrepancies in his initial impression. A web of tiny capillaries fanned across Hickok's cheeks. The whites of his eyes had a faint yellowish tinge, and the beginnings of a paunch showed above his gun belt. Leo's medical training suggested these were the marks of too much alcohol over too many years. It seemed Hickok's fast-paced life was catching up with him. For the moment, Leo couldn't remember Hickok's age.

Hickok glanced at Jacques, but only for a moment, then he took a business card from his shirt pocket and flipped it on the tabletop just as their waitress reappeared with his drink.

Hickok looked up at the waitress and said, "Hold on, little lady." He upended his wine and drained the glass in one long swallow, then handed it back to the girl. "Bring me another one, only this time put it in a man's glass, not a sewing thimble."

The girl blushed and departed quickly to get the marshal more wine.

Leo sipped his brandy as Hickok watched him through narrowed eyelids.

"I was wondering just what your card meant," Hickok said. "I never heard of a man being both a picture painter and a shootist."

Leo chuckled. "I've been told by some I'm a reasonably good painter of portraits. I'm not, however, what you have called a shootist. On occasion, I've settled differences between men by the use of a gun."

"You mean in a range war, or as a paid assassin?"

"Neither," Leo replied, toying with his glass, choosing his reply carefully. "I tend to be rather selective. I want no part of a shooting war where men take sides over some material issue, nor will I kill for the sake of money alone. As I'm sure you know, there are times when the weak are preyed upon by the strong, by men who are more skilled with firearms. In certain instances I have agreed to assist those who were unable to defend themselves against hired gunmen."

"Pardon my bluntness, Dr. LeMat, but you don't exactly look like a shootist to me." Hickok grinned, as if to take the sting out of his words.

"You look more like a city dandy than a gunslick."

"One might say the same about you, Marshal," Leo observed. "Appearances are often deceiving. Your dress is typical of a frontier scout or a man who fights Indians. I understand you've done both, however I would be hardpressed to describe you as a typical peace officer."

Hickok chuckled. "You got me there, I suppose. There are more than a few who think I dress wrong. Hell, I don't give a damn what folks think."

"You're not offended by their opinions?" Leo inquired.

Hickok leaned back in his chair to straighten his left leg. "Only if they get to funning me too much, and then I show 'em just why they dubbed me Wild Bill." Hickok's right hand flashed to his left side, and he drew one of his Colts. It was expertly done, Leo thought, as the marshal twirled the gun around his finger in a road agent's spin before he stuck it back in its holster.

Hickok's gaze moved to Leo's waist, then back to his face. "I see you don't even wear a gun, Dr. LeMat. Are you afraid somebody might call you out if you walk down the street with a pistol?"

"No, Marshal Hickok. I don't care what people may think of me or my appearance. But you're wrong when you conclude I'm not armed."

As the words left his mouth, Leo's right hand dipped inside his coat. In a blink, he drew his LeMat with the hammer thumbed back, aiming it at the roof of the veranda.

"Easy, Doc," Hickok protested. "That was plenty fast enough, I reckon. You can put that thing away. You made your point."

"Only a demonstration," Leo said, "meaningless unless a man can hit what he aims at." He lowered the revolver's hammer and returned it to his shoulder holster.

The waitress came back with Hickok's wine in a much larger glass, and bowed politely before she departed. Hickok took another drink and said, "That's better."

After a second healthy swallow, Hickok continued. "That's a real unusual gun you've got. Mind if I see it again? Can't say as I've ever seen one before."

"Certainly," Leo replied, handing over his LeMat revolver butt-first. "It was designed by my uncle, Colonel François LeMat, and machined by John Krider, a Philadelphia gunsmith of considerable reputation."

Hickok examined the piece, turning it over in

his hands several times. Then he gave it back to Leo. "Real unusual," he said again. "While we're discussing guns and shooting, did you see the attempted robber on yesterday's train from Fort Smith? I figure you came to Abilene on the Kansas and Pacific. One of the passengers shot two of the robbers stone-dead, according to the engineer. It was that bunch everyone's been calling Ghost Riders, on account of they wear white hoods and coats like they think it'll scare folks."

Jacques smiled, the puckering of his scar turning his grin into a curious leer. "Monsieur Leo shot one, and I took care of the other," he said.

Hickok seemed surprised. "I reckon I've lost a bet," he said.

"A wager?" Leo inquired.

"Yeah, with the part-owner of the Bull's Head Saloon, Ben Thompson. He bet me a man couldn't be a good painter and a good shootist."

"Perhaps you should wait until you see my painting before you call Mr. Thompson's bet," Leo remarked, drinking more brandy. "Let's order something to eat. We can discuss guns and painting with far more enthusiasm on full stomachs."

Hickok nodded, and Leo was certain that this Kansas marshal had a measure of higher respect for him now, after hearing the version of the train robbery described by Jacques, and witnessing Leo's speed drawing a handgun. Out here, much as in San Antonio, men were judged by different standards than they were in New Orleans.

He made a mental note to get a look at the infamous Ben Thompson while in Abilene. He'd heard of Thompson back in San Antonio, since the gunman was known to frequent Austin, Texas, during the winter. Thompson's reputation in Texas credited him with cutting a lethal swath through the saloon district in Austin, gunning down a number of men in barroom brawls, for which he was always exonerated by local authorities who said Thompson's actions were an acceptable means of population control, so long as his victims were deemed unsavory characters.

Chapter 9

Hickok appeared to be enjoying himself over a full platter of steak and potatoes, a dish of apple pie and three big glasses of wine. On occasions during their meal, Jacques gave Leo a disapproving glance over Hickok's table manners, for the marshal ate noisily, stuffing his mouth with food until his cheeks bulged, while making an assortment of noises—chewing with gusto, slurping wine and belching now and then. Leo observed Hickok's habits discretely, finding them both offensive and interesting, befitting the rough character he'd read about in *Harper's*, a man who spent most of his time in the wilderness scouting for the army or tracking down wanted men in order to claim the rewards offered for their hides, alive or dead.

Jacques offered no comment on the meal he ordered, although it was plain by the look on his face he held his cut of beefsteak in low regard. Nor did he seem any more appreciative of potatoes fried in oil without seasonings, or the rather tasteless slice of dried apple pie which lacked sufficient cinnamon, in his estimation.

Leo enjoyed his bowl of beef stew reddened with chili pepper and cumin, a distinctive combination of flavors he was unaccustomed to. His skillet-baked cornbread was sweetened with sugar, almost palatable enough to be called a dessert when drizzled with honey and butter.

"I'll sit for the painting, Dr. LeMat," Hickok said, pushing his empty plates away. "But I'm warning you ahead of time I'm not built to sit still very long. My nerves get the best of me sometimes."

"I promise to make each sitting as brief as possible," Leo told him. "However, to capture you on canvas the way I'd like to, I may need several days. The time can be of your choosing, either in the afternoon or later in the evening."

"I'll need to make it early," Hickok replied. "My job as city marshal keeps me busy at night. The big herds are coming up from Texas. We'll have drunk cowboys filling damn near every saloon at night, most likely before the week is out. I gotta do what they're paying me to do."

"I understand completely, Marshal. You can select whatever time you wish. I'll have Jacques supply you with your choice of red wines during the sittings. They won't last but an hour each day. Perhaps less.''

"I reckon I should be flattered that someone wants to paint me. Never had it done before. Plenty of tintypes have been taken of me for magazines and newspapers, but I never sat for a portrait." He tilted his head, wearing an amused expression. "I have to admit I'm puzzled by you, Dr. LeMat. A man who can draw and shoot a gun as well as you seem to be able to can make a good living in the gunman's trade. Painting pictures don't sound to me like it fits a man who's mastered a quick draw."

"As I told you before, I hire out my gun as more of a sideline than a profession. Over the years I've found it most difficult to ignore a request for help from someone who needs assistance when dealing with men who ignore the law. I must confess that I frequently enjoy putting lawless men in their proper place. It satisfies some inner need I have to right a wrong . . . to provide a balance when defenseless individuals are confronted by a bully, or a thief. I believe a great many men have a darker side, one that motivates them to take extreme risks. My blood courses through my veins when I face men with a gun. While it may sound like a poor way to describe it, I find the challenge of facing death both invigorating and somewhat frightening. It gives me a deeper appreciation for life and the things I often take for granted."

The marshal seemed bewildered by Leo's explanation. "Can't say as I feel the same way about it. I reckon I see it as just another way to make a dollar. It just so happens I'm good at it. I never bothered to understand why."

"Do you experience fear when someone challenges you?" Leo wanted to know. "Even the slightest trace of it?"

"I wouldn't call it fear. I get this tingling in my hands and fingers. It's more like being mad. I've never backed down from any son of a bitch . . . not one of 'em. I figure when it's my time to die, there'll be some gent who's a fraction faster than me. I haven't met him yet, and when the herds come in, this town is plumb full of gunmen and backshooters. I've got a wall full of wanted posters at the office. The crooks and hardcases show up here during the spring and summer to rob drunk cowboys of all their earnings. They used to get away with a helluva lot of it when Bear River Smith was county sheriff. But since I pinned on this badge, the worst of the gunslicks stay clear of Abilene. They know damn well I'll kill the sorry sumbitches if they try anything with me."

"I try not to fight when I'm angry, because anger inhibits clear thinking," Leo said. "But there are times I feel a touch of fear. When a man faces me with a gun, no matter who he is, I have a single objective . . . ending his life as quickly as I can."

The marshal chuckled. "You have a fancy way with words, Dr. LeMat. I reckon we're both saying the same thing. Some owlhoot thinks he can best me at the draw, and I'm real curious to see if he can."

"You're not afraid of dying?"

"Nope. Not in the least. We're all gonna die sometime or another, but Bill Hickok damn sure won't go down with his back turned to anybody. If I can't kill the son of a bitch, it's my bad luck. That's a chance I take whenever I go up against some shootist with a big reputation, but I'm damn sure not scared of him . . . don't matter who he is."

Now Hickok was curious. "How many men have you killed with a gun?" he asked. "Or is most of this just tough talk?"

"I don't count them," Leo replied. "It's a tragic thing to keep a record of, in my opinion."

Jacques spoke up when Hickok made a face, as if he did not believe Leo's answer. "Leo has killed more than twenty men in duels. I am certain of the number because I was present for all of them. There is easily another dozen who feed the maggots and alligators in New Orleans Parish and parts of southern Texas by Leo's hand, and the day before our arrival in this fair town, he added another to his list, as I told you before, a train robber who had the misfortune to board our private coach with a shotgun and lawless intentions."

Leo aimed a thumb in Jacques's direction. "My assistant has modestly omitted mention of the bravery in his own actions in the name of justice. As he himself said, Jacques killed a second highwayman who sought to relieve passengers and the railroad company's safe of their valuables. A ten-gauge shotgun at twenty paces makes a hell of a mess of whatever's in front of it."

The marshal regarded them both with a suggestion of doubt still creasing his face. "That's a lot of dead men. How come I've never heard of either one of you before?"

Leo debated his answer. "We've never found any reason to brag about it. It seems senseless to draw attention to killing someone. I think I speak for Jacques when I say neither one of us is particularly proud of it."

"If you hang around Abilene very long, you'll get a chance to test yourself against some of the deadliest gunmen west of the Mississippi," Hickok observed, apparently not quite convinced of Leo's or Jacques's ability with a gun.

Leo smiled, draining the last of his brandy. "I came here to paint your portrait, Marshal Hickok. I've no interest whatsoever in testing myself, as you put it, against men of that ilk."

Hickok pushed back his chair. "I'll be here tomorrow at one o'clock to sit for your painting. Make sure you have a bottle of wine, so I can be still for an hour. I hope this don't take too long. By the way, we've got an antigun law in Abilene, but I hardly ever enforce it anyhow. You can keep carrying yours under your coat."

Leo stood up and held out his hand. "I'm in your debt, and I assure you I'll keep my pistol hidden and do my best to finish the portrait as quickly as I can. Until tomorrow at one o'clock."

Jacques was bothered by something, scowling as Hickok rode away from the hotel.

"What is it?" Leo asked, placing several banknotes on their table to pay for the meal. "Something is troubling you."

"Hickok," Jacques replied, watching the marshal's back.

"What about him?"

"I'm not quite sure, *mon ami*. I may be wrong, but he is one man I would never turn my back on." Jacques hesitated, as if searching for the right words. *"T'es trop grand pour tes culottes."*

Leo gave a low laugh. "What do you mean he is too big for his britches?"

Jacques shook his head. "He is a showman, putting on an act to support his reputation as a killer. But I have my doubts he's as courageous as he believes he is."

Leo turned for the hotel doorway. "Nonetheless, he's an excellent subject. He gives every appearance of being a dangerous man . . . perhaps a bit past his prime, although as you have seen that his reflexes are still good. He handles a gun extremely well, with confidence. I must find a way to capture on canvas what he has shown us today."

Jacques followed Leo to the hotel entrance, paying scant notice to the cowmen and cattle buyers seated at nearby tables. "I suppose it does not matter," he said. "You've come here to paint his portrait, not to find out if he truly has the heart of a lion, as his reputation would suggest."

They started up a carpeted stairway to reach the third floor.

"He struck me differently," Leo admitted. "I think he's brave enough. Confident of his gunmanship. His age and poor health may be a factor in what you sensed about him, for I felt some of the same uncertainties about him. He didn't openly express his true feelings about facing men who were bent on killing him. Once or twice, his eyes betrayed him. I suspect he has doubts now, concerning his skills with a pistol."

"I wonder if he was ever as good as the stories say he was," Jacques remarked. "I've known men of his kind before, on the wharfs. They try too hard to convince others of their willingness to stare death in the face, but when the chips are down in the final game of survival, they rarely meet a challenge without being certain of having every advantage. I'll wager Mr. Hickok has seldom put himself into a fair fight."

As they reached the third-floor landing, Leo wondered if Jacques could be right.

Chapter 10

Sloan Wilson listened, resting one elbow on the bar at the Alamo, a foot propped on the bar's brass boot rail. The proposition Clyde offered interested him. He'd known Clyde for a number of years. Clyde Wall had a way of finding the right kind of work for men on the lookout for opportunity. Ever since Sloan rode into Abilene yesterday, he'd been wondering how to make a few dollars in this cow town on his way to the California gold fields. Clyde explained how the job made money, with a minimum of risk. It sounded easy enough. No one would recognize them in the outfits they wore—white flour sacks covering their faces to hide their identities while they stole cattle and robbed trains carrying big army payrolls. Clyde was describing how the gang conducted its business.

''We hit a couple of trains so far. Three of 'em, in fact. One had five thousand in gold in the safe. We blowed it all to hell with two sticks of dynamite."

"What about railroad detectives?" Sloan asked. Sloan was a cautious man, a habit that kept him alive in a number of dangerous occupations having to do with guns and gunplay.

"Wasn't any, until this last time. Some feller in a black suitcoat killed Shorty Russell an' Jim Bob Tucker. A feller was with him, wearin' a sailor's cap."

"A sailor's cap? It's a helluva long way from here to the closest ocean. What the hell was a sailor doin' on a train in the middle of Kansas?"

"I only got a glimpse of him. He showed up all of a sudden between two railroad cars with a shotgun. A little guy, hardly as big as a tick. Maybe he wasn't no railroad detective after all. Could be he was just a passenger with a goose gun. I got the hell away from there before I saw him real clear. He blowed Shorty clean off his horse. The tall gent killed Jim Bob when he tried to rob him. All I heard was this gunshot, an' then the sumbitch in the black hat an' coat throwed him off the train like he was a piece of rotten meat."

"Maybe the guy just got lucky," Sloan said. "I never saw a sailor who could shoot worth a damn. Some gents in the outlaw trade ain't careful enough. They don't last long. I just heard

Jim Hickok is marshal of Abilene. I know him. Somebody gave him a different handle to go by. Calls himself Wild Bill now, so I was told. Can't believe he's turned himself into a lawman. He'll kill a man in his bedroll while he's sleepin', if there's money to be made by doin' it. Don't show him your backside or you're liable to find a bullet hole through you."

"He's only a city marshal, Sloan. Got no jurisdiction over the railroads or cattle herds bein' held outside of town. All I ever seen him do is get drunk or put a crib whore in his lap. He don't strike me as bein' all that tough."

Sloan recalled his previous associations with Hickok, back when he was known simply as Jim, a farm boy from the Midwest who twirled a pistol on his trigger finger to attract attention from the ladies. He had scouted for the army, killing Indians up in Nebra'ra and farther north. Sloan knew Hickok as a cowardly sort who gunned down drunks and amateurs when he had a clear advantage over his adversary. "He ain't tough," Sloan agreed. "But don't let him get behind you. Now tell me somethin' about this man I'll be workin' for."

Clyde lowered his voice so other patrons inside the Alamo couldn't overhear him. "His name's Owen Bell. He comes from Mississip' . . . Natchez, to be exact about it. He figured to cash in on the boomtowns in Kansas Territory, buyin' up bunches of land where he was sure the new railroad lines would go. Gonna make a big profit off sellin' right-of-way to the rail lines, an' buildin' a cattle town at the end of it. Only everybody beat him to it. A bunch of bankers an' speculators got together an' built Hays, then they went further south an' west to build Newton an' Dodge City where ol' Fort Dodge used to be. Them railroad boys went plumb around Bell's land. Skirted him, so he never made a dime the way he planned. He claims it was a conspiracy, set up by a group of bankers an' big cattlemen with ties to the Kansas an' Pacific."

"He could be right," Sloan observed, tossing back a shot of flavored corn whiskey that burned all the way to his gut. "I've had a few dealin's with railroads . . . besides robbin' 'em a time or two. They paid damn decent money to work as guards aboard them baggage cars when the safe was full of valuables. Natural enough, I knew when a particular train was carryin' big money. Wasn't long till I seen there was more to be made by robbin' a train than guardin' what was on it."

"I've seen a few wanted posters out on you, Sloan," Clyde said, "only they never had no good description. One of 'em said you held up the Rock Island an' Pacific. They was offerin' a thousand dollar reward on your head."

"That was back in Missouri, nearly ten years ago. I kept movin' on after that. A thousand dollars is enough for a man's own mother to turn him over to the law. Me an' the gang split up an' went down to Texas for a spell. Trouble was, the damn Texas Rangers are the meanest bunch of lawmen who ever got astraddle of a horse. Some of 'em's nothin' but hired killers themselves. I got the hell outta there soon as I got word they was lookin' for me."

"I never tangled with no Texas Rangers, but I've heard they can be real rope-happy. Shorty tol' me he was down in Texas when Buster Cox got caught by a posse of Rangers south of Fort Concho a ways. They strung ol' Buster up to the only tree in fifty miles. Didn't give him no trial or nothin'. Shorty claimed he saw it from a cave on the Concho River when his horse got crippled. Right after that's when Shorty hightailed it out of Texas to this hellhole. He said it was safer here, away from them Rangers. That was before that sawed-off little bastard in the sailor's cap blowed him away. I reckon if Shorty could talk, he'd say Kansas didn't turn out to be so safe after all."

"Whose idea is it to wear white sacks over your head?"

"Mr. Bell's. Only they ain't sacks, really. They's some sort of costume for a real secret organization, so Bell claims, called the Knights of the Golden Circle. Them silk hoods got a little green snake sewed on 'em."

Sloan nodded, beckoning a bartender over to refill his glass. "I know plenty about the Knights," he said, waiting until the barman brimmed his shot glass and moved out of hearing range with Sloan's silver coin. "One big bunch of 'em is headquartered in Natchez Under the Hill. They hired me to kill a man one time, right after the war was over. The Knights have got plenty of big money behind 'em. Rich men, mostly Confederate sympathizers who ain't done fightin' the Union. They hired me to kill a carpetbagger judge in Vicksburg who was takin' away Southerners' land by court order. The head man of the Knights in Natchez paid me fifteen hundred dollars in gold to kill Judge Piner, half up front an' half when the job was done. I put a hole plumb through that judge's brain one night while he was drivin' home in his fancy black buggy. He wasn't even carryin' a gun. Easiest money I ever made. An' I know all about them pointed silk hoods with a little snake stitched into 'em. I never seen the man's face who hired me to kill that judge. He wore a hood an' a fancy silk cloak both times he paid

me. We met in an upstairs office behind the
Crystal Palace, off this alley in nearly the roughest part of Natchez. Two men with shotguns
kept an eye on me the whole time I was there.
They wore the same kind of outfits."

"Jesus, Sloan. Sounds kinda cold-blooded to
me, killin' that judge. It ain't that I'm set against
killin' somebody when I have to, but I've never
took money for murderin' an unarmed man. But
like you said, fifteen hundred in gold is a helluva lot of cash. You're just the man Mr. Bell's
lookin' for, no doubt about it. He's payin' three
hundred a month an' a share of whatever we
can rob from cow herds, or a train. We use a
runnin' iron on the longhorns we rustle an' sell
'em to this gent from Council Bluffs. He don't
ask no questions 'bout them altered brands
'cause we sell him the cows cheap."

"Sounds good to me," Sloan said. "Take me
to meet this Mr. Bell. I don't want Hickok to see
me. He'll know about them rewards out for me
an' he's just liable to get drunk enough to try an'
claim 'em. I'd have to kill him if he tried it, an' I'd
have to clear out of Kansas in a helluva hurry."

Clyde gave him a sideways look before he
drained his shot glass. "You fast enough to kill
Wild Bill Hickok?" he asked, like he wasn't sure.

"Ain't no doubt about it, Clyde. Hickok was
always fast when he was sober. Trouble was, his

aim wasn't none too good. Some claimed it was bad eyes. Remember one thing about goin' up against some feller with a gun: It don't matter who fires the first shot, if it's wide of the mark. Makin' sure you kill the son of a bitch in front of you is all that counts. Back when I knowed Jim Hickok, before they took to callin' him Wild Bill, he couldn't hit the side of a barn with a fast draw if he was standin' more'n a few yards away. He's plenty fast, only he just can't shoot straight over no distance."

Clyde looked over his shoulder. "He'll be headed down to this part of town pretty quick. He starts drinkin' early, I hear tell."

Sloan pushed away from the bar. "Bring my horse around to the back. It's the red roan with a pitchfork branded on its flank. I'd just as soon Hickok didn't know I was in town."

"I'll fetch your horse. We'll ride out to Mr. Bell's place by the back way. I'll tell him I can vouch for you, 'cause we done plenty of jobs together a few years back. If you know of anybody else who can handle himself in this line of work, he'll draw the same wages . . . only whoever he is, he's gotta be good, an' he's gotta know how to keep his mouth shut."

Sloan looked out at the street through the Alamo's batwing doors a moment, thinking, ignoring the sun's harsh glare. "I did see Carl

Pickins camped outside of Fort Scott last week. He said he was headed this way, bein' real careful to avoid them army patrols on account of the rewards out on him. He'd be a damn good man to have sidin' us in a fight."

"Carl Pickins?" Clyde whispered, glancing around the room to be sure no one heard him. "I was told he got shot to pieces in that bank holdup in Springfield . . . thought he was dead."

"He ain't dead. I talked to him last week. He's still got buckshot in his side from that bank job. Made a helluva mess outta his face, but he damn sure ain't dead. He said he jerked some kid off a mule while all the shootin' was goin' on an' rode down this alley behind the bank. Got away clean, only he told me he was laid up in bed for two months till his wounds healed."

Sloan noticed Clyde was frowning.

"I ain't so sure 'bout Pickins, Sloan," Clyde said quietly. "He's plumb crazy. He likes the killin' part. I joined up with Frank Dalton's bunch down in the Nations for a spell, an' that's where I met Carl Pickins. We robbed that stagecoach out of Fort Smith. Dalton said the strongbox held money bound for a Denver bank. We had the job pulled without no trouble, an' then Carl turned his shotgun on the women an' children passengers. He shot every one of 'em dead, Sloan, when there wasn't no need. Killin' women an' children just ain't my style. Pickins got this scary look on his face an' started shootin', reloadin' and shootin', till they was all dead. Dalton couldn't stop him. Pickins said we wasn't leavin' nobody alive who could identify us."

Sloan found Clyde's concerns downright unusual. "I can't see nothin' wrong with makin' sure there wasn't no witnesses. In case it slipped your mind, robbin' trains an' stagecoaches can get a man a helluva prison stretch if he gets caught. You're gettin' soft, Clyde. Workin' for this Bell feller, if we find ourselves in a tight spot with the law or the army, I'd damn sure feel better havin' Pickins backin' us up."

Clyde turned to fetch the horses. "Whatever you say, Sloan, only I sure as hell will be hopin' Carl don't decide he wants my share of the loot."

Sloan watched Clyde saunter out of the building as if he had no particular place to go, turning for the hitchrail where Sloan had tied his horse.

Three hundred a month, Sloan thought, *and a piece of whatever we steal. It won't take me but a few months to build up a grubstake for the ride to California.*

Sloan saw his reflection in the mirror behind the bar, a square face covered with dark beard stubble, a flat-brim hat pulled low in front, its crown encircled by loop of Mexican silver con-chos. He doubted if Hickok would recognize him now, even if they did pass each other on the streets of Abilene by happenstance.

I'll kill him if he causes me any trouble, Sloan promised himself. *Unless Hickok has changed his ways with a gun, it'll be easy.*

Through a window of the Alamo, he saw Clyde riding a bay away from the hitching post, leading his strawberry roan. He waited a few seconds longer and then strolled across stained floorboards to go outside and around to the back.

The dirt streets of Abilene were busy, crowded with wagons and mounted cowboys. No one would pay him any notice in the midst of so much activity.

Walking toward the rear of the building, he remembered his brief association with the Knights of the Golden Circle. They could be dangerous to double-cross. Men with enough money behind them could hire the best assassins around, men who wouldn't care about how or where they killed their victims. If Mr. Owen Bell had the right connections with the Knights' se-cret organization, he could have damn near any-one put in a grave.

Sloan wasn't all that happy about wearing a

robe or a hood when they pulled a robbery. But if the pay was right, he'd do it.

He mounted his roan and followed Clyde Wall toward what he hoped would be a golden opportunity.

"Let's swing through Deviltown," he told Clyde. "There's a whore down there called Flat Nose Kate. Carl will stop by to see her on his way through. I'll leave word for him to hang around a day or two, that there might be some good-payin' work. He'll know to lay low so Hickok won't know he's in town. Prob'ly stay at Maude's Boardin' House durin' the day."

Chapter 11

Leo was at work before his easel, roughing in charcoal lines that would become Marshal Hickok's face, working from memory of their first meeting and the tintype resting on the bottom of a nearby chair. His shirtsleeves were rolled up to facilitate the movements of his wrist and hand, while in his mind's eye he saw Hickok as plainly as he had on the veranda of the Drover's. His imagination recreated small details he'd been taught to pay close attention to by Catlin: deep folds of an eyelid, creases across a forehead, wrinkles traveling from the corners of a mouth and the exact outline of the lobe of an ear. Attention to even the slightest detail, Catlin would say, is the difference between a truly magnificent portrait and a talentless attempt by the hand of an untrained, unschooled observer. Leo made the tiny marks that would remind him to capture those subtle features found in Hickok's face.

Jacques was downstairs in the kitchen, arguing with the cook over the use of a small corner of one of the hotel's giant iron woodstoves so that he could prepare one of his specialties tonight—a meatless gumbo requiring only vegetables and rice. Jacques had packed a wide selection of his own seasonings. This was Jacques's second argument of the day with hotel cooks. Asking to prepare a pot of chicory for their morning's enjoyment had been, according to him, an insufferable ordeal since no rooms at the Drover's had stoves. Guests in the wintertime had to settle for the unreliable services of a steam boiler out back, with heat piped into tiny radiators in every room.

A rapping on the door interrupted Leo's concentration on his work, and he put his charcoal down reluctantly before he got up. His gun and holster hung from a peg beside the door, within easy reach if his unexpected visitor proved to be unfriendly . . . not that Leo expected any such thing in a place where he was not known by anyone.

"Who is it?" he inquired, a precaution before twisting the doorknob.

"Sheriff Roy Jones, Dr. LeMat. If you can spare a minute I'd like to ask you about what happened on the train. I've got a few questions."

He opened the door. A graying man approaching sixty years of age, slightly overfed, wearing a stained gray felt Stetson and tweed trousers over his boot tops, offered his palm, while his fleshy jowls widened in a poor attempt at a smile. "Roy Jones," he said in a nasal voice. "I'm sheriff of Dickinson County. A woman at the hotel desk gave me your room number an' told me you was here. Hope you ain't real busy."

Leo shook with him, paying quick attention to the Colt .44 belted around the sheriff's ample waist. "Leo LeMat," he said, opening the door wide. "Please come in, Sheriff Jones. I'm not too busy to answer your questions."

Jones walked into the room, immediately noticing the easel and canvas. "You a picture painter?" he asked. "Somebody told me you was."

"I paint portraits. Take a chair over by the window and then tell me what you wish to know about the robbery."

Jones swaggered over to a vacant chair and sat down, pulling off his hat and resting it on the floor beside him. "I talked to the conductor about what happened, but I wanted to hear your side of things. I was told you shot one of the bandits when he came into your private railroad car, an' that your partner, some little feller with a name the conductor couldn't pronounce, shot the other gent with a shotgun. Is that more or less what happened?"

Leo nodded. "The first fellow entered my car and demanded our valuables. He was aiming a shotgun at us. I pretended to reach inside my coat to hand over my money. I carry a pistol in a shoulder holster. What I gave the would-be robber was a lead bullet. I was completely within my rights, and I have a witness to what took place."

"I wasn't meanin' to imply you didn't have no right to kill him," Jones explained. "Just wanted to get the facts straight, is all."

"My associate, Jacques LeDieux, will return shortly to tell you about shooting the second robber."

"I'd have trouble sayin' his name right myself. Your word's good enough, Dr. LeMat. To tell the truth, I'm glad you got two of 'em. Only I'm puzzled why you didn't let the train crew bring the bodies back for identification. I was hopin' somebody would know who they was. This is the first time somebody actually got any of the bastards."

"They were a fairly bloody mess after we shot them, Sheriff, and nothing either Jacques or I said to the train crew would have prevented the bodies from being brought back. It was merely a suggestion on Jacques's part that they be left where they fell to feed the buzzards. Apparently, the crewmen aboard the Kansas and Pacific wholeheartedly agreed."

"We've had plenty of trouble out of these Ghost Riders, as folks have taken to calling them. They've robbed two trains in this part of Kansas, an' run off with nearly six hundred head of cows. Them two's the first to get caught in the act. I've had a posse out lookin' for 'em several times an' can't find hide nor hair of 'em. It's like they up an' disappeared. Me an' a deputy rode east early this mornin' along the Kansas an' Pacific tracks to get a good look at them two corpses. Wasn't much to look at. Wolves already got to 'em before we did."

"I would have expected no less," Leo said. "Scavengers are naturally drawn to the scent of food, and they make no distinction between upright creatures or those of the four-legged variety. Did you find anything on their persons which might help to identify who they were?"

"I picked up one of their hoods," Sheriff Jones continued, gazing absently out a window. "Bloody as hell, with a hole right between them two eye holes. I found one thing that puzzles the hell outta me . . ."

"And what was that, Sheriff?"

"There's this real small green snake, all wound up like it was gonna strike, embroidered into the bottom of the cloth. I never seen such a thing before. I was wonderin' if you had any idea what that snake stands for. Looks to me like it oughtta mean something."

"Quite simple," Leo said, returning to his chair in front of the easel. "It is the symbol for a secret society known as the Royal Order of the Knights of the Golden Circle. It is known in some regions as the sign of the coiled serpent."

The sheriff blinked, staring at Leo for several seconds before he spoke again. "What the hell is a Knight of the Gold Circle?"

"The *Golden* Circle, Sheriff. It is a fraternal organization of sorts, dedicated, among other things, to preserving the notion of racial superiority of whites over negroes and other races. It flourishes in the South and parts of the Midwest. It was founded in Ohio, I believe. They exist in groups, according to geography, if I recall my readings on the subject correctly. Some are far more radical than others. They have been known to resort to violence to get what they want; however, I have never heard of them being involved in outright robbery or cattle theft, as you have described."

"Then what the hell is that little snake doin' on the hoods I found?"

Leo leaned back in his chair. "Quite possibly someone only wants people in this area to think these are the illegal actions of a renegade group of the Knights. I'm merely venturing my best guess."

"But you said they could be violent . . ."

"They have been involved in some racially motivated hangings and a number of chilling murders, according to newspaper accounts I have read. Very little is actually known about them, since as I told you before, they hide their identities behind masks. No one can be certain who is a member of their secret organization, unless one of them comes forward to publicly proclaim some tenet of their beliefs."

"Some what?"

"Some racial policy they believe in. That's really about all I know regarding their reasons for existence. Perhaps a U.S. Marshal might be able to tell you more."

"I reckon I can wire Fort Smith. Judge Isaac Parker's court is in charge of the United States Marshals for some parts of the Western District. I'll mention what you told me about them Gold Knights in my telegram about the robbery attempt to the marshals' service."

"Knights of the Golden Circle," Leo said again, in hopes that Sheriff Jones would remember it all the way to the bottom of the hotel stairs.

Jones nodded and stood up. "Trouble is, we

ain't got nary a soul I can think of who'd be involved in nothin' like that. I'd bet damn near half the cowboys we get up from Texas is negroes, Meskins or half-breed Injuns. Cowboyin' ain't a job all that many men want in the first place, don't matter what color they are." He picked up his hat and returned it to his head, apparently finished with his questions.

"As I suggested before, Sheriff Jones, someone may only be trying to *appear* to be representing the Knights. Robbing trains is not, as I understand them, the ordinary business of Knights of the Golden Circle. I'd do some checking around before I placed the blame on their organization. It doesn't sound like what I've read about them in the past."

"I'm obliged, Doctor. By the way, I hear you had a talk with our city marshal, Bill Hickok, today. A feller told me you had lunch with him downstairs."

"I came here to paint his portrait," Leo explained. "He is, in many quarters, a very famous man."

Jones pulled a sly grin as he headed across the room for the door. "He can sure shoot the hell outta stray dogs. In case nobody told you, he shot one of his own men durin' a big disturbance we had last year. Killed him. Hickok claims it was an accident."

"I take it you're not particularly fond of Hickok," Leo said pointedly. He made a mental note to learn more about the incident.

"We don't get along too good. He acts like the gun ordinance don't matter, an' a cowboy up from Texas damn near has to shoot somebody in cold blood before Hickok will arrest him. He plays real smart politics."

"He also has quite a reputation, particularly when it comes to his gunmanship."

"He's good, all right," Jones agreed, placing his palm on the doorknob. "When he's sober."

"You believe he's a heavy drinker?"

"Some'd call him a drunk. But he's real popular with the saloon owners an' the whores. He leaves 'em pretty much alone to do their business."

"And you don't approve?"

"I ain't sayin' that, exactly. It's just that when we've got a law, it oughtta be enforced, like the one that says no guns can be carried in town."

"I missed seeing the sign posting the ordinance," Leo said. "I must have had my mind on other things," he added, recalling the lovely Pauline.

"It ain't hardly there no more. Got shot so full of holes by drunk cowboys you couldn't read it no ways. What damn good is a sign if nobody can read it?"

"A good point, Sheriff."

"Thanks for your time, Doctor. I'll get off that wire to Fort Smith makin' mention of what you told me 'bout them Golden Circles. Maybe they know what the hell they are."

Leo showed the sheriff out and closed the door. There was no mystery now as to how a gang of robbers could operate in the county without being apprehended. Meeting Sheriff Roy Jones had explained everything.

Leo went back to work at his easel.

Chapter 12

Jacques was in utter despair, pacing back and forth in front of their hotel room windows with his hands clasped behind him, an angry scowl pinching his face. "These cow country cooks, if they can be called cooks, are complete idiots! I doubt they would be capable of opening a tin of peaches without assistance."

"Calm down, my friend," Leo said, facing the wall to hide a grin while fastening his shoulder holster and donning his coat and hat. "We can eat whatever fare they have to offer. While I agree some of it will be less than palatable, my bowl of stew was quite delicious. Chili pepper makes a nice addition to an ordinary meal."

Jacques would not be persuaded. "It was, in all likelihood, an accident," he snapped, continuing his march from one window to another. "Some dolt probably bumped into another cowboy who had a tin of chili powder in his hands.

It had to be a spill, not an actual recipe. All I asked for was one corner of a stove and a cast iron skillet. A toothless fool with a scruffy gray beard ordered me out of the kitchen, insisting it was *his* kitchen because he was the head cook. Indeed! I gave some thought to having him taste the tip of my Bowie's blade, to see if he could recognize the flavor of his own blood." He glanced at Leo when Leo reached for the door-knob. "Where are you going, *monsieur*?"

"To find a place called the Bull's Head Saloon. As you heard during our lunch with Hickok, Ben Thompson is one of the owners, and he is in town. I want to get a good look at him. I have read about his exploits in Austin. He is reported to have shot down at least a dozen men in Texas and somehow, all charges were dismissed against him. I must see him in person, and this is my first opportunity."

"I'll never understand your fascination with these Western gunmen, Leo. As we have both learned, they are no more skilled in the art of killing than most of the land-bound pirates we fought along the wharfs of Breton Sound, or the backstreets of New Orleans. If there is a difference, these cowboy types are bolder, prancing about wearing their big hats and their pistols in plain sight, as if to proclaim their manhood. Given a choice, I would prefer to face any of these cowboy gunmen I have seen so far, rather than walk down a single dark alley near Canal Street after midnight."

Out of habit, Leo opened the door, making sure the hallway was empty. "You overlook the most important distinction. Men like Hickok or Thompson face their enemies in contests of skill and daring. The back alley thieves and robbers we knew as young men are, for the most part, cowardly sorts who kill from hiding or when a man's back is turned. There is a significant difference, *mon ami*, one that makes legends out of rather ordinary men to the readership of Eastern newspapers and magazines. Or, as in the case of Ben Thompson, a man with a fearful reputation in his own surrounds. These are the men the public wants to see on canvas, for the printed word has made them seem larger than life to a great many people."

Jacques was clearly still in a foul mood over his disagreement with the head cook downstairs. "I'm sure you'll be as disappointed with Mr. Thompson as I was with Marshal Hickok. It seems a waste of perfectly good oils and canvas to paint their portraits."

Leo was reminded of his earlier visitor. "While you were downstairs, Dickinson County Sheriff Roy Jones came to see me, to inquire as to the circumstances of the train robbery and the men we killed. I described the events as they took place. He rode back to get a look at the bodies. Not much was left behind thanks to wolves, he said. He asked about the coiled serpent he found on one of the white hoods. I told him as much as I could recall about the Knights of the Golden Circle. He'd never heard of the organization before."

"What is this sheriff like?" Jacques asked. "Does he seem capable of finding the other robbers?"

"I doubt it. Jones appears to be a tired old man who does not care much for his job. He also holds Bill Hickok in very low esteem. The way Jones described it, this town is torn apart by two factions: its peaceful citizens, and businessmen who want to keep the cattlemen's trade. Hickok caters to the businessmen, allowing all but the most flagrant violations to go unnoticed and unpunished. Sheriff Jones also repeated what you told me before—that Hickok shot one of his own deputies during an altercation last year. The man died. Hickok insisted it was an accident and no charges were filed."

"I'm not surprised," Jacques said. "After meeting Hickok in person, I'm all but convinced he is something of a fraud. Like the insolent bastard who confronted me in the kitchen."

"I'll be back before long," Leo said, hoping to

avoid any further discussion of Jacques's frustration by stepping into the hall.

"Should I go with you in case Mr. Thompson has a few dangerous friends?"

"It won't be necessary, Jacques. As I told you from the beginning, I've come to Kansas to paint these men, not to challenge them. While I'm away, have a glass of wine and stop this fretting over the use of a hotel stove. We'll manage to survive their primitive cuisine somehow."

He closed the door quickly, just as Jacques opened his mouth to begin what was certain to be another heated discourse about the quality of food served at the Drover's Inn.

A boy sweeping the front porch of an establishment called McCoy's Drover Supply and Hardware directed Leo toward the Bull's Head, in a section of town known as the Devil's Addition. Well away from the center of town, rows of shabby false-fronted saloons and gaming parlors crowded together on two dusty streets pockmarked with deep chugholes. Though it was still early in the afternoon, dozens of saddled horses were tied in front of a number of saloons. Somewhere in the district, a piano player with absolutely no ear for music attempted a rendition of "Camp Town Races."

The Bull's Head was one of the larger clap-

board buildings in Devil's Addition. High atop
a wooden storefront, an artist with even less talent than the poor piano player had painted a
huge longhorn bull above the doorway, along
with a crudely lettered sign with the establishment's name. As an obvious afterthought, perhaps
to keep from offending a more discriminating clientele, the bull's testicles had been covered by
a thin, almost transparent layer of whitewash.

As Leo strolled toward the Bull's Head, he
attracted the notice of a few cowboys lounging
on shaded porches in front of smaller saloons.
Most of them carried guns in outright defiance
of Abilene's city ordinance. It was Leo's finer
apparel that made him a curiosity in this section
of town, he felt sure, and perhaps also the fact
that to all outward appearances he was not carrying a sidearm.

It was an act of mercy, he thought, when the
distant piano player finally ended his off-key
tune. Frederic Chopin, were he still alive, would
most certainly have marched over to the spot
with a shotgun to end this form of unforgivable
abuse employing his favorite instrument.

He came to the saloon's swinging doors cautiously, peering over the tops before walking inside. The room smelled of stale sweat, cigar
smoke, and beer.

Three cowboys occupied a table in one corner

of the place, their hands filled with playing cards. Otherwise, the Bull's Head was empty. Each of the cardplayers made a show of turning to watch Leo enter, and none of their faces appeared friendly.

He crossed over to the bar, where a lone bartender gave him a critical eye.

"What's for you, mister?"

"Do you sell Kentucky sour mash whiskey?" he asked, deciding against brandy in a place like this since the quality of it was sure to be lacking.

"It's four bits a shot," the barman replied. "Most of our customers can't afford it."

"I assure you I have the price. Please pour me a glass and I'll show you the color of my money."

The barkeep reached under his bar to bring out a bottle of branded whiskey, Old Rocking Chair, a label Leo recognized. He dropped two silver quarters on the countertop, feeling the stares of the cowboy gamblers on his back.

A slightly smudged shot glass was filled, then the bottle corked. Leo tasted it, wondering how much water had been added to stretch it. "Perfect," he said, although he truly felt otherwise when a suggestion of tobacco for flavoring crossed his tongue. "Don't put it away. I may have several more."

The bartender smiled. "Them's mighty nice

duds you're wearin', stranger. Don't get many
men dressed like you in this end of town. What
brings you?"

"I'd like to make the acquaintance of Mr. Ben
Thompson. I understand he is a part owner of
the Bull's Head, and furthermore, that he is
presently in Abilene."

The smile left the barman's face. "What business have you got with Ben?"

"None whatsoever. Marshal Bill Hickok made
mention of Mr. Thompson while we were having lunch. Apparently, the two of them are
friends. I only wish to meet Mr. Thompson and
nothing more. I presently reside in San Antonio
and I understand he spends the winter in
Austin."

"You know Wild Bill?"

"We've just met. We will have several more
meetings while I'm in Abilene."

"What business have you got with Wild Bill?
Are you one of them Eastern newspapermen
who come to hear his story?"

"I'm not a journalist. I paint portraits of famous people, and Marshal Hickok is my present subject."

"You don't look like no painter to me."

"Looks can be deceiving, my friend. Now, is
it possible for me to meet Mr. Thompson?"

"He's in the back. I don't see no gun on your

hip, so I reckon it'll be okay if I tell him you're here. Didn't catch your name."

"Leo LeMat. Dr. Leo LeMat."

"You're a doctor too? Maybe you can help me," he went on, lowering his voice. "I've got this problem with . . . my privates, if you know what I mean. Got it from this whore. I got sores all over down there. This sawbones here in Abilene said there ain't no cure."

"It's known as the Pox in most circles. Syphilis is the medical term for it. Alas, I fear the 'sawbones,' as you've described him, is correct. There is no known cure."

"I'm gonna die then, ain't I?" He said it in a whisper as beads of sweat rapidly formed on his brow.

"Not immediately," Leo replied. "The sores will continue to spread. A solution of potash to the afflicted areas may help you suffer less, and certain tinctures of arsenic have been known to slow down the disease's progression. Pus will form, a constant annoyance. In later stages your vision will grow worse. You may lose a few teeth and experience some problems with your cleft palate . . ."

"My what?"

"The roof of your mouth. Sores will develop there too."

"I'm gonna kill Kate, that lousy whore. She

gave it to me, and a bunch of others down in this end of town. I'd be within my rights to shoot the bitch.''

"It seems too late for retribution. Try the potash and tincture of arsenic to ease your discomfort. There is little else you can do, other than taking laudanum when your pain worsens.''

"I *am* gonna shoot the bitch!" he growled, no longer whispering. "I'll go get Ben, then I'm gonna find that goddamn whore an' blow her head off.''

"But wouldn't Marshal Hickok arrest you for murder?" Leo asked, more interested in the barman's answer than the actual result.

"Hell no! Not if it was just some lousy whore who gave me the Pox. Kate's the same as dead right now. Wait here, Doc, an' I'll tell Ben you're here.''

A cowboy from the gambler's table spoke up. "Don't you be killin' no whores in Abilene just yet, Casey!" He chuckled. "In case you ain't got no calendar, there'll be five or six hundred woman-hungry cowboys hittin' this place over the next few months, an' whores is gonna be in short supply.''

Everyone at the table laughed while Casey went through a door into a back room. Then, as Leo finished his drink, another gambler asked a question.

"Did I hear you say you was a doctor?"

Leo took a deep breath and turned toward the table. "I am, although I no longer practice the healing arts. I wonder why you ask?" He tried not to let his irritation show.

"I got this itchin'. Little bugs crawlin' all over parts of me. Got it down in the Nations while we was bringin' our herd north."

"When did you first notice it?" he inquired, deciding that for the sake of meeting Ben Thompson without causing a disturbance in his saloon, he would play along with the drover.

"Can't say for sure, Doc. Seems like it was a couple days after I humped this Osage squaw. Traded her a sack of tobacco for what she had under her deerskin dress."

He watched the cowboy scratch his crotch through his denim trousers. Now, instead of irritation, Leo felt amusement. "You have what is clearly a serious case of Indian body lice."

"Injun body lice?" the man wondered aloud. "Didn't know there was more'n one kind."

"Indian body lice, especially the variety carried by the Osage tribe, can be fatal if not properly treated, and soon."

"You mean it could kill me?"

"It can be a slow, painful death."

The cowboy stood up abruptly, tossing down

his cards. "What the hell's the treatment, Doc? I gotta know!"

"Fire," Leo told him with practiced calm. "First, you must burn all your clothing. Every stitch of it, and all your bedding as well. Time is of the essence. Were I afflicted with Osage body lice, I would run behind this very building and set fire to everything I was wearing, including my hat. The longer you wait, the more certain death becomes. Minutes may count."

"But I'll be plumb naked in broad daylight!"

"Do you wish to live, my friend?"

"Hell, yes I do. But everybody who sees me is gonna laugh at me."

"Better to have them laugh than attend your funeral. After you burn your clothing, hurry down to the closest apothecary shop and purchase a bottle of Butler's coal tar liniment. Cover your entire body from head to toe with the solution and wear no form of clothing for twenty-four hours. You'll be cured, if you act in time."

"Shit," the drover muttered, unbuttoning his shirt while hurrying for the batwing doors as his companions broke into fits of laughter.

Chapter 13

A mustachioed man wearing a dark red vest and a starched white shirt with a fresh cardboard collar and string tie emerged from the back room, giving Leo a doubtful glance, hesitating in the door frame while keeping his right hand near a cross-pull holstered Colt pistol. A derby hat rested at a jaunty angle atop his head.

"Are you the painter Hickok told me about?" he asked, his voice deep, throaty.

"It's possible," Leo replied. "I came to Abilene to paint his portrait. I wrote to him in advance. I am Dr. Leo LeMat."

"I'm Ben Thompson. Casey said you wanted to talk to me."

"Only to meet you, Mr. Thompson. If I've come at a bad time . . ."

"I wasn't busy. Curious, more'n anything else. Bill showed me your business card. It said somethin' about you havin' a gun for hire."

"Possibly a poor choice of wording, Mr. Thompson. I am not what you might consider a hired gun in the traditional sense. I hoped to make the card simple, easy to understand."

Thompson came forward to the rear of the bar, offering his hand. "Nice to meet you, Dr. LeMat. The name strikes a chord with me from the war. You any kin to the LeMat who invented that pistol with a shotgun barrel in the middle of the cylinder?"

"My uncle, Dr. François LeMat. I carry one of the smaller version of his guns." He took Thompson's handshake.

Thompson let a grin cross his face. "Casey tells me you're also a physician, an' that he's gonna die of the Pox. He ran out the back with a scattergun, swearin' he was gonna kill some whore named Kate livin' in the cribs."

"It was only a guess, based on what your bartender told me regarding his condition. If it is the Pox, sadly, there is no cure. I hope I won't be held responsible for a murder if he shoots the woman."

"He shoulda kept his pants buttoned up round these damn whores. My first cousin carried a LeMat pistol in the war. He was with Hood's Texas Brigades at Franklin, Tennessee. Only Confederate officers could get their hands on one. He was a captain in the cavalry. He showed us one of your uncle's pistols after he got back from Tennessee. Damned good idea, when you've got buckshot in a handgun to use at close range."

"The invention made my family a great deal of money over the years; however it is no longer in production. One has to learn how to carefully load the center barrel with gunpowder and shot. Otherwise an explosion may occur. Some have reported losing fingers when an improper loading is performed."

"Casey said you lived in San Antone, but you don't sound like any Texan I ever knew. You've got a real strange accent when you talk."

"I was born in New Orleans."

"I reckon that explains it. What was it you wanted with me?"

"Merely to make your acquaintance. As Marshal Hickok may have told you, I am here to paint his portrait."

"Yeah, he told me about you when he showed me your card. I bet him money a man couldn't be a real shootist and a painter of good pictures. One or the other, is what I said. Are you any good with a gun? Don't seem you're wearin' one."

"I carry a LeMat revolver under my coat. I see no point in flaunting the antigun ordinance here in Abilene, however I rarely go anywhere without it. Old habits are hard to break."

Thompson seemed puzzled. "Why in the hell did you want to meet me? I'm no dime novel hero like Hickok."

"You have earned your own deadly reputation in Texas, Mr. Thompson. I intend to paint several portraits of the West's most notable gunmen. I wondered if you might sit for me."

"You mean sit still while you paint my picture?"

"It's quite simple, really. All you do is sit."

"I don't reckon I'd be interested, Dr. LeMat. First off, I ain't lookin' for any more notice than I already get. When you get a reputation with a gun, there's always some young tough who thinks he's faster an' wants to prove it against you. Makes it hard to avoid trouble when I go someplace. Too damn many folks already know what I look like down in Austin. Up here, it ain't so bad. There's plenty of fast gunmen to go round."

"I'm merely asking you to consider it," Leo said. "Perhaps sometime when you're in Austin, we can arrange a meeting."

"I'll have to think about it. I've had a few tintypes made of me, but that don't take but a few minutes."

"I understand. Possibly later on. I'll leave one

of my cards with my address in San Antonio. I'll be leaving Abilene as soon as I complete Marshal Hickok's portrait. While I find this town an interesting place, full of unusual characters to say the least, I have no further business here."

"It can get a little rough durin' cow season, 'specially in this end of town. See all those bullet holes in my ceiling? If it rains, this place leaks like a flour sifter."

Leo noticed the hundreds of holes in the roof of the Bull's Head and his curiosity got the best of him. "Why do you allow customers to shoot holes in your roof?"

Thompson grinned, lifting the ends of his dark brown waxed mustache. "It's just cowboys lettin' off steam, mostly. It's when they shoot holes in each other that I put a stop to it. If you look at the floor, you'll find a few old bloodstains along with tobacco juice when some gent misses a spittoon."

"You don't rely on Marshal Hickok's help when customers get out of hand?"

"No need. I can handle 'em as well as Bill. Maybe better, when he's had too much red wine."

Leo continued to study Thompson's face and mannerisms while the saloon owner talked. Not as physically impressive as Hickok in many respects, Ben Thompson had an air about him, radiating the confidence shown by men who had been tested in tough situations. Thompson would make an excellent subject for a portrait of a gunman, although he did not dress the part of a typical Westerner. There was a message behind his eyes, an unmistakable warning to those who meant to cross him. "I've been told Hickok drinks quite a bit, yet he seems to have been able to handle his job in a tough town."

Thompson was amused. "Most cowhands are scared of him, because of his reputation. Ain't many who'll try him these days."

Leo sensed that Thompson knew Hickok's skills were on the decline, though he did not come right out and say it. "He has captured the imaginations of Easterners who read what has been written about him."

"Yeah. But even Bill will tell you a lot of it's nothin' but bullshit. As a joke, he told a writer from back East that he'd killed a hundred men. The guy believed him an' wrote all about it in some magazine. Bill thought it was mighty damn funny, how that fool believed him so quick. Most folks are sure gullible as hell. Once a story gets started, it gets better every time somebody tells it. Folks around here have even come to believe in ghosts who ride horses an' rob trains. I don't reckon you've been here long enough to have heard that one."

"Indeed I have," Leo replied. "In fact, my associate and I killed two of the train-robbing ghosts on our journey to Abilene this week. It should help dispel rumors they were not mortals."

Thompson gave him a riveting look. "I heard Bill say two of 'em got shot to hell at the Gates Center water stop. I didn't know you're the one who did it. I've been tellin' Bill all along those boys wear disguises 'cause somebody'd recognize 'em if they didn't. It's some local bunch, only they sure as hell know when a train's got money on it, or when a herd of cattle ain't bein' guarded too close. It's my idea those sheets are uniforms of the Ku Klux Klan. Only a damn fool believes there's such a thing as ghosts."

"Both men we shot wore silk hoods and robes bearing the insignia of a coiled serpent, worn by members of the Knights of the Golden Circle."

"I've heard about 'em," Thompson replied. "We've got a few over in East Texas, only they ain't near as well known as the Klan. Bat Masterson told me they're damn near the same thing, but there ain't as many of the Knights, he said."

Leo nodded. "I understand most of them are in the Old South and parts of the Midwest. Kansas seems an unlikely place to find an organization dedicated to maintaining the racial superiority of white men, and I've never heard of them being involved in the robbery of trains or cattle rustling."

"I don't know hardly anything about 'em, Doc, but most anybody in Abilene could be one, I reckon. This town is new. Folks come from everywhere to try an' make a slice of the money bein' made in the sin trades or the cattle business here. The two go hand-in-hand. Durin' the high part of cow season we got crooks of every description—cardsharps, pickpockets, backshootin' thieves who rob drunk trail hands, medicine peddlers who sell flavored whiskey an' big promises. You name it. The only thing we're short of round here is preachers and honest men."

Leo chuckled in spite of the obvious truth behind Thompson's words.

Their conversation ended abruptly when the roar of a shotgun blast echoed from farther down the street. Thompson glanced to a front window, seemingly unruffled.

"Sounds like Casey found the right whore," he said, without any noticeable emotion.

"Will Marshal Hickok investigate?" Leo asked.

"Not likely. If Bill investigated every gunshot he heard in this end of town, he'd be worn down to a frazzle. Besides, no one is gonna care if somebody kills a sick whore once in a while. A thing like that can be real bad for business. Word spreads down the Chisholm that we've got sick whores an' the herds will swing over to Hays, or Dodge. A few sick crib whores can ruin a good cow town. Besides, if Bill was to arrest Casey, he'd swear his gun went off accidental. Maybe he tripped over an empty whiskey bottle. Casey can round up a dozen witnesses who'll take an oath that it's the truth."

Leo found Thompson's detachment from a cold-blooded murder hard to stomach. "I appreciate your time, Mr. Thompson. Here's my card. If you change your mind about having your portrait done when you're in Austin, please contact me by wire at the Saint Anthony Hotel." He placed a card on the bar.

"Pleased to make your acquaintance too, Doc. Like I told you, my cousin Frank sure was proud of that LeMat pistol he had durin' the war. Claimed it was the best gun he ever owned."

As Leo strolled out of the Bull's Head, he saw a crowd of curious people gathered around a door in a row of tiny rooms at the outskirts of the Devil's Addition. Walking over, he saw the bartender named Casey standing there with a shotgun balanced in one hand, peering into one of the cribs. Leo was aghast. Was he in any way responsible for the woman's death? He told himself he'd merely given Casey his medical opinion for an ailment the bartender described. He couldn't have known this would send Casey on a killing spree.

A senseless execution, and I am not at fault, he decided, turning for the center of town until he noticed a curl of black smoke coming from a vacant field behind the saloons.

A naked man tended to a small fire topped off by a smoldering cowboy hat, his back turned to a group of men watching the odd proceedings. Leo could hear gales of laughter coming from the bystanders.

"I'll run fetch a jug of that coal tar, Cody," someone said from the back of the growing crowd.

"Bring me a clean bedsheet," Cody whimpered, casting worried looks around him. "I don't give a damn what that sawbones said. I ain't gonna go plumb naked till tomorrow . . ."

Leo made his way out of the saloon district, confounded by most of what he'd seen and heard. Ben Thompson was a man to be feared by lesser individuals. He judged it would take uncommon skill for a gunman to bring Thompson down. And Leo's opinion of Abilene's seedy residents had reached a new low, after learning that an afflicted bartender could commit murder in full view of the sin district's residents without facing the consequences of the law. Leo's only uplifting moments had come when the gullible cowboy made a spectacle of himself by setting fire to his attire in public. However, his real lesson in the treatment of body lice was yet to come. Unless he washed the coal tar solution off his skin within a matter of minutes, he would soon feel as though he'd caught fire himself, a fact that would surely occur to him when the pain became unbearable.

Leo made up his mind that what he needed now was a decent glass of brandy, possibly several, and enough time to forget about the decadence he'd found in Abilene's Devil's Addition.

Jacques sat across from him on the veranda of the Drover's Inn watching traffic move up and down the street.

"You seem distracted, *mon ami.*"

"I suppose I am. This visit to Kansas has taught me several things about mankind in general. Lower forms of human life are not confined to the slums of New Orleans or larger cities. They are drawn by one common factor: the easy exchange of money for pleasures of every description. The setting for these events makes no difference, so long as it is tolerated by the authorities. In its own crude way, this place is no different than the foggy waterfronts of our youth, albeit lawlessness is overlooked here in broad daylight. I find it a rather sad commentary on the growth of man's greed and his potential for corruption."

"I can have our trunks packed and be ready to leave as soon as I contact the stationmaster about coupling our coach to the next train leaving town," Jacques offered, all too eager to depart.

"No, my friend. We are not leaving until I have captured Hickok on Canvas."

"We may starve before then," Jacques sighed. "Only a man with a strong constitution could survive on the slop we're being fed. If, as you say, lawlessness is being overlooked in this town, do not be surprised if the cook at this inn is found cut into small pieces one morning, floating in a kettle of his own miserable soup."

Leo laughed, reminded of his plans this evening when he saw a black carriage drive by. "I'll be careful not to order the soup," he said. "Besides, I have an appointment for dinner with a beautiful woman tonight. Let's retire to the bathhouse with a bottle of brandy while we soak away this dust. I'll have someone at the hotel desk hire a carriage for me at six o'clock, so Miss Pauline Matlock and I can tour the countryside before supper."

Chapter 14

Clyde sat his horse on the south bank of the Solomon River in the shade of a cottonwood grove, resting his elbow on his saddle horn. Sloan Wilson, slumped in the saddle, waited beside him on his red roan.

Clyde watched the log house on a rise north of the river for several minutes, making sure the prairies around them were empty.

"What the hell we waitin' for?" Sloan asked.

"Makin' damn sure nobody sees us. The boss don't like it if we ride up to the house in broad daylight."

"What kind of feller is this Bell?" Sloan demanded angrily. "How come we can't just ride in?"

"He's a real careful man, Sloan. He was a spy for the Confederacy durin' the war an' he don't like no carelessness."

"How long we gonna sit here?"

"Till I'm sure nobody's around. It looks okay. Let's ride over. The river's shallow here—hardly touches a horse's belly, if you know the right spots."

They urged their horses into the shallows. Beyond the river a herd of antelope watched them from a grassy hilltop.

The house was a rambling affair, its rooms strung out in a line, railroad style. Barns and empty corrals sat in back of the place, where a windmill pumped water from deep within the depths of the flinty soil.

Clyde wondered how Mr. Bell would take to Sloan. Sloan was gruff, rough-edged, unlike the bossman's polite but cold manner.

"We'll ride around to the back," Clyde said. "Hide our horses in them barns."

"I ain't keen on all this sneakin' around, Clyde. If this feller wants to hire my guns, there's no reason I have to act like I'm not good enough to come in his front door."

"Think about the money, Sloan. What damn difference does it make what door we have to walk through to collect it?"

"It just don't set well with me, havin' to sneak in the back way. But like you say, all we really give a damn about is the money."

*   *   *

Owen watched them through his army field glasses at a window facing south. "I warned Clyde," he muttered, speaking to a heavy mulatto cradling a shotgun in the crook of a thick arm. "Do you recognize that fellow with him, Moses?"

"No sir, I sho' don't. Clyde wouldn't have brung him here if he didn't have no good reason."

"Whoever he is, I hope he knows what he's about. I'm tired of employing worthless saddle bums who can't shoot, men without nerve. Bring them to my study, Moses, and keep a sharp eye on the newcomer."

"I'll blow him clear to hell's front door if'n he touches a gun," Moses promised.

Owen entered a dark room with heavy curtains covering the windows. He lit a single lantern, pausing when light struck a banner on the wall behind his desk.

"Sons of Liberty be damned!" he hissed, admiring the coiled snake sewn into the banner of gleaming gold silk. It galled him when someone said the Knights had been disbanded by a fool named Clement Vallandigham to form the Sons of Liberty, after the fall of the Confederacy. What did a stupid Ohio politician know about men sworn to secrecy in the name of a just cause?

Emblazoned above the coiled serpent were the words "Knights of the Golden Circle." Owen found it ironic; when most of the country believed the Knights were no more, they had become even stronger—not in numbers, but in dedication to their secret society.

He sat down, awaiting Clyde's arrival and the identification of the stranger with him. Tenting his fingers over his desktop, waiting, he considered two new troubling thoughts. If the Grand Master in Natchez found out what he was doing—using the robes of the Knights as a way to disguise his personal quest for revenge—no doubt someone would be sent to kill him. The Royal Order was never to be used for personal gain or profit, upon penalty of death.

And there was more troubling news coming from Abilene in regard to the men killed during the railroad robbery. Some tall stranger calling himself Dr. Leo LeMat had informed Sheriff Jones of the origins of the sign of the coiled serpent. Now Jones was asking everyone in town if they knew anything about the Knights. Whoever this mysterious Dr. LeMat was, he apparently knew how to shoot, for young James Matlock had been all too willing to tell Owen about LeMat's version of the holdup failure and his role in it. LeMat had to be silenced before he told too many people what he knew about the symbols found on the dead men's robes. Jimmy said LeMat was a portraitist, an individual who shouldn't be all that difficult to kill. After all, how skillful could a painter be with a gun? His success halting the train robber was most certainly a piece of luck.

Jimmy Matlock had proven useful. Unlike his more civilized father, Jimmy longed for a life of excitement. While he could never be completely trusted due to his tender years and brazen manner, he had become a valuable source of information regarding the arrival of cattle herds in Abilene. Perhaps without fully realizing it, he was giving Owen things he needed, relying on the empty promise that one day, Owen would bankroll him in a venture of his own in Dodge City.

He heard spurs rattling across floorboards at the back of the house, pushing thoughts of Jimmy Matlock from his mind. On the other hand, Jimmy's beautiful sister rarely ever completely left Owen Bell's thoughts. Under the right circumstances, at some point in the future, he intended to have her for his bride. He knew very little about the lovely Pauline, and could only just stare at her when he saw her in town. But it was quite obvious she liked the finer things Owen could provide—pretty dresses, the finest imported French perfumes—and she seemed to enjoy traveling by rail.

I'll take her to see the sights in San Francisco, he thought as heavy boots approached his study. Just one or two more army payroll robberies, along with the sale of stolen longhorns, and he would recover his losses from a bad investment in the wilds of Kansas. The loss was, no doubt, the result of a conspiracy by Northern bankers and former Union sympathizers turned railroad men to leave him bankrupt.

Moses stuck his head through the door. "It's Clyde, an' a man calls hisself Sloan to see you, sir."

"Send them in."

Chapter 15

Chief Deputy U.S. Marshal Heck Thomas entered Judge Isaac Parker's chambers with a telegram in his fist, a wire that had reached Fort Smith only minutes ago. "Got somethin' to show you, Judge."

Judge Parker gave Thomas a haggard, red-eyed stare. It appeared as if he'd been awake for a day. "What is it, Heck?" he asked.

Thomas nodded to George Maledon, a towering Bavarian who served as Judge Parker's executioner. Maledon was known in some quarters as the "Virtuoso of the Rope" for the number of hangings he had performed on behalf of Parker's court. In a few short years on the bench, Parker had sent twenty-six men to the gallows, Thomas remembered, and they all died by the hand of the Bavarian.

Maledon stood motionless in a corner, saying nothing to acknowledge Thomas's silent greeting.

"It's a telegram from the Dickinson County sheriff over in Abilene," Thomas began. "He's askin' if we know anything about the Golden Circle of Knights."

Parker sighed, taking the telegram. "I'm sure he means the Knights of the Golden Circle." His gaze wandered down the paper. "Surely this sheriff knows we have no jurisdiction in Kansas Territory. He should have wired Kansas City."

"I hear Roy Jones ain't got a helluva lot of sense, Your Honor. Marshal Ault knows him, an' he said Jones never wanted that job in the first place. All them cow towns over in Kansas are big trouble while the herds come in. Abilene hired ol' Bill Hickok for city marshal. He's liable to get drunk an' kill the mayor himself, if he takes the notion. They found a fox to watch the hen house, if you ask me. Jones is also askin' if we ever heard of a doctor by the name of Leo LeMat. As you know, I'm from Texas. LeMat hails from New Orleans, by way of San Antone. I know considerable about him. Even met him on a couple of occasions."

Parker looked up from the wire. "And who is this Dr. Leo LeMat?"

"Real strange feller. He paints pictures, but I don't figure that's why he's in Abilene . . ."

"Go on, Heck. Tell me about LeMat. This telegram merely asks what we know about him."

"He's a hired killer, only nobody's ever gotten the goods on him, far as I know. I was in San Antone when he killed two men. I've knowed Sheriff Wheeler down there for some time, so I asked him about the killin's, and about Doc LeMat. Wheeler claimed LeMat was clear of any charges. He baited Doyle Allison into drawin' on him first. LeMat killed him with one shot, an' Doyle Allison was no slouch with a pistol. Doyle was wanted for murder down in Galveston, so LeMat collected a five-hundred-dollar reward. Allison's pardner, a backshooter named Billy Roberts, tried to gun LeMat down from an alleyway. Roberts missed, an' LeMat shot him dead. Collected a hundred in reward money for him. If Doc LeMat's in Abilene, you can bet your last dollar he's there to kill somebody. He damn sure ain't there for the scenery. Wheeler also told me that LeMat still engages in old-fashioned duels over one thing or another. It's still legal in Bexar County if you register with the county judge beforehand."

"A savage practice," Parker commented. "However, none of this has anything whatsoever to do with this court. You can wire the sheriff, telling him what you know about the doctor, and you may add that the Knights of the Golden Circle no longer exist. They came to ruin after the fall of the Confederacy. He wouldn't have found any of the Knights in a primitive outpost like Abilene in the first place, for there is no more slavery and, I suspect, precious few negroes. This Roy Jones is either mad as a hatter from inhaling too much mercury vapor, or he has a drinking problem every bit as severe as Hickok's is reported to be. Answer this telegram if you wish. If it were left up to me, I would simply toss it in my wastebasket."

"I'll send him some sort of reply, an' I tell him to keep an eye on LeMat. My gut tells me there's a killlin' in the makin' in Abilene, with Doc LeMat in town. Maybe you never heard of 'em, but LeMat's kinfolks invented this peculiar gun . . . a pistol, only it had a second short barrel that fired a powder charge behind a load of buckshot. Marshal Evett Nix used to carry one. He said even when he was drunk, he couldn't miss with the buckshot if he got close enough."

Judge Parker lifted one eyebrow. "Marshal Nix admitted to drinking while on the job?"

Thomas grinned. "He never said he was wearin' his badge when he hoisted a few too many. I reckon you'd better ask him about the circumstances yourself."

"Nix is an excellent peace officer, although I understand he went through some wild years in his youth. He came to me highly recommended for his marksmanship, and his honesty," Parker said thoughtfully. "To be perfectly honest about it, when I was given this judicial assignment, I soon learned the wisdom of fighting fire with fire. Arkansas and Indian Territory had become a haven for the bloodiest cutthroats and outlaws anyone could imagine, as you well know from personal experience here. When men like Nix went out and captured them by whatever means, I felt I had a duty to hang the miscreants to prevent them from doing more harm. It is a policy I shall continue as long as I remain on this bench, although at times I grieve over the lives I have ended, despite the obvious necessity of it."

"I'll get an answer off to Sheriff Jones," Thomas said as he went to the door. "I'll tell him what you said about the Knights of the Golden Circle bein' gone, an' I'll add what I know about Dr. Leo LeMat."

Parker halted him with a final question. "Is Dr. LeMat truly a medical doctor?"

"So I was told. He wasn't practicin' when I was down in San Antone. It was more like he meant to go into the undertakin' business."

Chapter 16

They sat in high-backed cast iron bathtubs, surrounded by warm, soapy water. Leo and Jacques had the bathhouse to themselves. A young girl with Indian features brought them pails of hot water from time to time. Leo lathered his cheeks and used a straight razor to rid himself of his beard stubble, pausing long enough to sip more brandy until he was satisfied with his appearance in a small, handheld mirror.

Jacques puffed on a rum-soaked cigar. "This is a very poor substitute for the Saint Anthony," he grumbled. "At least we had baths on every floor."

"How quickly you have forgotten your primitive beginnings. I knew you when you had no bathtub at all. In those days I was always careful never to stand downwind from you during the winter when the bayous were too cold for swimming."

"I have not forgotten, *mon ami.* A surly chuck wagon cook with no teeth or a razor has spoiled my day. I am still giving serious thought to carving him into stew meat tonight while he sleeps."

Leo was enjoying his friend's sour mood, for he knew it was only a passing thing. "I'm asking you to resist such urges. I rather enjoyed the stew here. It had a nice flavor . . . subtle, without too much spice."

"An accident, as I said before. I hate this place, and this miserable town. I hope you can capture Marshal Hickok on canvas to your satisfaction in the shortest possible time. Abilene can be appropriately named a city of fools, built by the droppings of cattle."

Leo swallowed more brandy. "I find this city, if it can be called a city, as repugnant as you do—not so much for the town itself, rather for its low-bred inhabitants. A prostitute was slaughtered in the middle of the afternoon in the Devil's Addition while I was there, and by all appearances, nothing will be done about it. The culprit will be allowed to remain a free man simply because his victim was a poor fallen dove afflicted with a social disease."

"We saw whores with their throats cut all over the French Quarter when we were boys, Leo. No one did anything about it then, either."

Leo remembered. "I suppose I have become more civilized, after my medical education. What I saw today offends me, not so much for the loss of a woman's life, but for the public indifference to it. It sickened me."

"Like the food here," Jacques said, blowing smoke toward the ceiling. "Would you have as much compassion for me if I were to strangle to death on a tough steak at the Drover's Inn?"

Leo didn't bother to explain the difference, instead turning his thoughts to an evening with Pauline. "One thing this Kansas prairie produces is remarkably beautiful women. Miss Matlock is but one example. She has a certain quality I find hard to put into words."

"I'm sure you'll attempt to seduce her tonight," Jacques said. "While you are displaying your most charming side to the young woman, I'll find something to do. I had planned to prepare a grand gumbo for you and your lady this evening, until I ran afoul of that insolent cowhand wearing an apron who dares to call himself a cook. I should have cut out his tongue when he ordered me out of his kitchen. One swipe of my blade and he would be with his ancestors now. I've killed men for less."

Leo knew Jacques spoke the truth. Despite his small size, Jacques had a fearsome reputation in the rougher sections of New Orleans, and had

Leo not intervened by taking him away to Texas, in all probability Jacques was headed for prison, or an early grave at the hands of men who sought revenge against him for some misdeed. "Allow me to plead for a return to your peaceful side until we leave this town. We have traveled halfway across this continent to apply oils to canvas. Killing a chef over a tough piece of meat and tasteless potatoes seems too vengeful to fit the nature of the crime."

"A small corner of his stove for an hour was all I asked him for. I should have killed him when I had the chance . . ." He ended his tirade when they heard soft footsteps in the hallway leading to the bathhouse.

The Indian girl returned with two steaming buckets of water, and she carried them to Jacques's tub first, smiling at him. She wore a plain blue cotton dress and worn sandals.

"You need more hot water," she said, pouring a pail slowly into his tub.

Jacques looked over the woman's pretty face. "Thank you," he said. "My name is Jacques LeDieux. What is yours, if I may ask?"

"I am called Ann. I am Cherokee. My Cherokee name is Anatoka. The man I work for, Mr. McCoy, gave me a name he said was easier to remember."

"Anatoka. It's a beautiful name. It has a note

of music in it. I like the sound of it—it is very pleasant to the ear. I would have no trouble remembering it."

The girl blushed and lowered her eyes. "And you are called Jack?"

"That's close enough." He looked her up and down a moment, as though trying to make up his mind about something. "If you have no plans for dinner this evening, I'd be honored to take you somewhere to eat, just so long as it is *not* at this hotel. The food here is intolerable."

The girl's flush only deepened. "Mr. McCoy says I cannot be seen in the company of hotel guests. It is a rule that must be followed by anyone who works in this bathhouse. I am so sorry, Jack."

"He would never have to know," Jacques persisted. "We could arrange to meet somewhere, a place of your own choosing where the food is not so bad."

"I am afraid he would find out. I would go hungry without this job. Almost no one in Abilene will hire an Indian girl like me."

"We could go someplace quiet in another part of town. We could share a bottle of good wine or perhaps some peach brandy along with our meal."

"I do enjoy the sweet taste of peach brandy."

She gave Leo a wary look. "No one can know about it. Mr. McCoy would be very angry."

"Let me suggest this, Anatoka," Jacques continued, pressing his slight advantage. "Meet me behind the inn after dark. I'll bring peach brandy and cheese and a loaf of fresh bread. You can show me a place where we can talk and be alone. In the dark, no one will see us together."

"I suppose it will be okay, Jack. I'll change into my best dress. I only have two . . ."

"Then it is agreed, Miss Anatoka. We meet behind this bathhouse after the sun goes down."

She nodded and hurried over to add the remaining pail of hot water to Leo's tub. She couldn't look at him, as though she wished she hadn't made the arrangement with Jacques in Leo's presence.

She hurried out of the bathhouse without saying another word, carrying her empty buckets.

"Ah, *mon ami*," Leo said quietly. "It would seem you also have plans for the evening."

"Do you find her pretty?" Jacques asked.

"Indeed. Her skin is like darkened cream with a hint of light copper hues, as smooth as velvet. And she has beautiful eyes."

"Yes, she does," Jacques agreed. "She said she has only two dresses. With your permission, I would like to draw against my wages, only a small amount, enough to buy Anatoka a dress befitting a woman with her charms."

"Done," Leo answered. "Buy her two dresses, and a decent pair of shoes."

"I did notice her sandals. She is obviously quite poor. I wonder why her employer is so strict about having her accompany a guest of the hotel?"

"A house rule, I suppose. Or Mr. McCoy, whom we have not met, may only be interested in protecting his investment from the improper advances of wandering Frenchmen, who would steal her away from his employ."

For the first time since his disagreement in the Drover's Inn kitchen this morning, Jacques smiled. "The same could be said about Mr. John Matlock regarding his concerns for what a physician-turned-painter from San Antonio wishes to do to his lovely daughter. He may be rightfully worried about your less than honorable intentions, suspecting that you intend to violate Miss Pauline."

"I would never rob a woman of her chastity, Monsieur LeDieux. However, if she were to give it up willingly, that would be an entirely different matter."

"You will ply her with wine, sweet words, and a gentleman's charm."

"Those are not weapons of war, my friend. I will merely treat her like a lady."

"I know your methods well, Alexandre LeMat," Jacques said as he climbed out of the tub to dry off with a towel. "I have seen you when you were all too willing to refill a woman's wineglass until she fell out of her chair."

"I protest my innocence!" he replied. "How can I be at fault when a young woman appears to be thirsty?"

"It was never a woman's thirst you meant to satisfy, Dr. LeMat."

Leo got out of his tub, applying a towel to his wet limbs and hair. "I dare say the fair Cherokee maiden who brought us our bathwater is in far more danger of being violated tonight than is the daughter of John Matlock. As a man of some refinement, I will not tempt Miss Pauline with an offer of new clothing and shoes in order to take her to bed. I will rely solely upon my limitless charm to win her heart."

Jacques shook his head, pulling on clean trousers while he spoke. "Mademoiselle Matlock's heart is perfectly safe while in your company. Other parts of her anatomy will not be so well guarded, I fear."

"You offend me with your baseless charges. Say no more, or I shall be forced to remind you of an incident in New Orleans in which a wharf rat named LeDieux was caught in a most compromising position with a city policeman's wife while the poor man was on duty."

"Enough," Jacques muttered, pulling on his boots. "I wish you the best of luck tonight."

Leo slipped into a clean starched shirt. "And I wish you the same good fortune in your efforts to defile the Cherokee princess. However, I feel compelled as your friend to leave you with a parting thought. Have you ever wondered what it would be like to be scalped?"

"You can be a heartless scoundrel at times, Leo," Jacques told him.

He handed Jacques the bottle of brandy. "I may be nothing but a scoundrel, my friend, but let's drink to our mutual success tonight."

"May the better man win," Jacques toasted, before raising the bottle to his lips.

"May *both* of us win," Leo suggested, when the brandy was given to him.

They left the bathhouse together to climb the stairs. As they reached the stairway, Jacques cast an evil glare into the dining room.

"Have you ever eaten what some cattlemen call 'mountain oysters'?" he asked.

"Not that I remember. What are they? Oysters are only found at the bottom of the seas."

"Fried cow testicles," Jacques replied, starting up the steps. "A satisfactory substitute may be the balls of a man who calls himself a cook for cowboys. I'm tempted to experiment with a new delicacy tomorrow. I'll work on the recipe tonight.''

Chapter 17

Leo found the house easily enough in a quiet part of Abilene's northern section, where white-washed plank homes with shaded summer porches sat far from the noise of saloons and the stench carried by winds from the cattle pens. A blazing red sunset lit the prairies west of Abilene, painting the hills with varying shades of scarlet and deepening gold and casting shadows where homes and stunted trees were neatly arranged on grassless dirt yards.

He halted the canopied surrey and climbed down, wearing his best split-tail frock coat and black pants tucked into the tops of his stovepipe boots. A splash of rose-scented hair oil kept his locks in place when he removed his flat-brim hat. A bottle of Martel lay hidden beneath the buggy seat, along with a light comforter, for with the approach of sundown a slight chill had come to the air.

He climbed the porch steps and rapped gently on the door with his hat in his hand. Moments later, John Matlock answered his knock, offering a handshake.

"Come in, Doc. Pauline's almost ready. By the way, how did your meetin' with Marshal Hickok go this afternoon?"

"He agreed to sit for his portrait," Leo replied, shaking the cattle baron's palm briefly. "He's an interesting character. Quite pleasant, in fact, although I wouldn't care to find myself facing his bad side, which I understand surfaces more frequently when he has been drinking."

Matlock showed him into a well-kept front room with upholstered furniture and polished end tables. "Have a seat. She won't be but a minute . . . You know how women can be. As to Hickok and his temperment, he can be a bully at times. Mostly when he's drunk, like you said. But when he's drinking, he keeps mostly over in the Devil's Addition."

"I saw part of it today," Leo said, taking a chair near the front door, resting his Stetson over a bent knee. "It appeared to be rough enough to suit Marshal Hickok's tastes when he has the urge to demonstrate his willingness to entertain any form of difficulty with rowdy cowboys."

"He ain't known for bein' bashful about it,"

Matlock agreed as the swish of soft fabric came from a hallway leading to the front of the house.

Pauline came into the room, her auburn hair done in ringlets, a hint of rouge coloring her cheeks. She wore a bright yellow dress with a lacy white shawl over her shoulders. "Good evening, Dr. LeMat," she purred, favoring him with a wonderful smile, enjoying the steady look he gave her. "I'm ready now."

Leo had come to his feet. "You look lovely this evening, Miss Matlock. I've hired a surrey in the hope that you will be willing to show me the sights around Abilene. I brought along a lap comforter, for I fear it may be cold when I drive you back home after dinner."

"How thoughtful of you, Dr. LeMat. I'm afraid there aren't many sights to see. However, I'll do my best to point out what few attractions we have."

John Matlock scowled. "Just be sure you stay wide of that sin district, my dear. Stray bullets have been known to fly all over that end of town."

"Of course, Dad." She gave her father a peck on the cheek and walked to the front door as Leo opened it for her.

Matlock was still frowning when Leo went down the porch steps with Pauline on his arm.

* * *

"I don't think your father cares for me," Leo said as they drove past the western outskirts of Abilene. A darkening sky encroached upon a horizon tinted by the last rays of pink sun.

"He has never liked any man who paid me a social call," she replied. "We've argued about it. He is far too overprotective of me. We had a terrible fight before he agreed to let me ride the train alone to visit my sister and her new baby. At the last he reluctantly gave in. I don't think he'll ever let me grow up on my own."

The click of the chestnut buggy horse's iron shoes added to the rattle of iron-rimmed wheels over the flinty ground. "He loves you, Pauline. It's understandable that he'd want to keep you from harm."

"He goes too far at times. I'll be twenty-one next August, and if Dad continues to keep me locked in a closet, I'll die an old maid. I don't even have a regular beau. He won't allow it."

"He agreed to let you have dinner with me this evening," Leo said.

"Not without a struggle. At first he refused to let me go, not until he'd spoken with Sheriff Jones about you. He wanted to know something about your background before he consented to let us spend time together. He's too old-fashioned, and I told him so in plain language this afternoon."

"Plain language?"

She smiled. "I called him an old fuddy-duddy and went to my room, slamming the door in his face. I threatened to run away from home without telling him where I'm going, unless he allows me more freedom to live my own life. My sister got married to a young minister whom she initially despised, just to get away from our father. Fortunately, my sister Elizabeth has since fallen in love with Eugene. He has been a good husband to her, though he is a poor provider. A minister in this godless cow country has difficulty making ends meet."

Leo swung the buggy horse toward the highest hilltop west of town, which would give them a view of Abilene as lights brightened windows across the city. "Not many cowboys are inclined to tithe in support of a church when they rarely go inside one. For your sister's sake, I hope the preaching business in Abilene picks up as time goes by. We'll stop at the top of this hill for a time to see the lights. It's chilly, but I brought a bottle of brandy along, in case you feel cold."

"A small amount of brandy would be nice," Pauline agreed.

Her movement was slight, scarcely noticable, when she leaned ever so gently against his arm.

Chapter 18

Carl Pickens would be the first to admit that he didn't know beans about horseflesh. The clay-bank dun he rode into Abilene in the murky darkness right after sundown was just about the ugliest animal he'd ever seen—high withers, a thin ewe neck and a Roman nose, with the roughest gait he'd ridden lately. But a footsore man on the run, faced with the necessity of stealing a horse in the dark, couldn't afford to be picky. Riding out of the Indian Nations before a posse of U.S. Marshals from Fort Smith caught up to him made a more critical selection of a getaway horse far too dangerous. The dun had been the first gelding he came across in a farm-er's field, after his sorrel became wind-broke southeast of old Fort Scott. Spurring relentlessly to stay ahead of the posse, he'd ridden his sorrel to death near a farming community east of the Kansas line, and had few choices other than boosting this horse. Better to have saddle galls on his thighs than a hangman's noose around his neck, he reasoned at the time.

He rode slowly through deep shadows close to shacks behind the Devil's Addition, with a meaty hand resting on the butt of his Mason Colt .44–.40. Beneath his moth-eaten duster, a Stevens 10-gauge shotgun dangled from his left shoulder on a leather strap, its barrels sawed off to a mere twelve inches. The gun would spread a pattern of molten buckshot so wide it would fill a pair of stable doors from hinge to hinge. Inside Carl's shirt, a .32-caliber Remington belly-gun was tucked behind his belt. He also carried a sixteen-inch Arkansas toothpick in a sheath sewn into the stovepipe top of his right boot, and a .44-caliber Smith & Wesson derringer in a scabbard hidden in the other boot. Carl Pickins believed in the value of weaponry, vowing never to be the victim of an assassin's bullet for lack of the means to shoot back, or a chance to slit his enemy's throat if all else failed.

He rode to a ramshackle barn behind Maude's Boarding House and unsaddled his horse, turning it into a small corral. With his saddle and war bag over his shoulder, he stepped cautiously to the back door of the boardinghouse and let himself in.

A woman in a greasy apron saw him enter

the kitchen at the rear of the place. She stared at him a moment. "Is that you, Carl Pickins?" she asked.

"It's me, Maudie. Need a place to sleep an' a bite of food."

"You got four bits? I want the money in advance, Carl. I let you off last time, on account of you was hurt bad. Jesus! Them pellets made a mess outta your face . . ."

"I got the money, Maudie. Fix me a plate, an' tell me what room I get upstairs."

"Nine's empty. A feller moved out last week, owin' me four dollars. Put the money on the counter, Carl. I can't afford to be so generous this time."

He dropped his saddle and gear on the floor to fish a fifty-cent piece out of his pants. "You're a cold-hearted ol' bitch, Maudie. I was gonna pay you anyways."

"Like hell. I ain't runnin' no damn charity round here. You've run out on me before without payin'."

"I was drunk that time." He placed the coin on her washstand. "After I eat I need to talk to Kate. I forgot what crib she's in."

"She ain't in none of 'em no more, Carl. She's dead."

"Dead? What the hell happened to her?"

"Casey Kelly, bartender over at the Bull's

Head, blew her face off this afternoon. Worst sight I ever saw. He claimed she gave him the Pox."

"I'll kill the son of bitch! Kate was a friend of mine," he snarled, jutting his jaw.

"I'd give that some real close thinkin', Carl. Ben Thompson is in town. He won't take it kindly if you try killin' his best bartender. Ain't but two men in this town I'm scared of. One's Ben. The other's Bill Hickok. Flat Nose Kate may have been a real close friend, but I'd think twice before I went over to the Bull's Head after Casey."

Carl feared Thompson more than most men he'd ever met. Down in Texas one time, he'd seen Thompson fast-draw Cotton Proctor and lift him right out of his boots before Cotton could clear leather. "I ain't all that scared of Hickok," he said, relaxing the angry fists he'd made of his hands.

"You oughtta be," Maude said, going back to the carrots she was cleaning over a dishpan. "Bill ain't no match for Ben, but if I was you I'd stay away from both of 'em."

"I'm gonna get even with that Casey feller. I'll lay for him somewheres one of these nights. Won't nobody but me an' him that know who done it."

Maude wagged her head against the idea. "Put your gear up in number nine an' then come downstairs. Beans is still warm on the stove, an' there's cornbread left. Buttermilk's outside in the springhouse, if you want, only you'll have to go down an' fetch it yourself."

Carl bent down to pick up his saddle and belongings. "I met up with Sloan Wilson a few days ago. He said he'd leave word with Kate where he'd be."

"He stopped by here middle of the day. He was with Clyde Wall," Maude remarked, scraping a carrot with her knife. "Said to tell you if you showed up, to stay put. He said somethin' about havin' work for you."

"I remember Clyde," Carl said, omitting any details of their previous association. "If Clyde or Sloan shows up, tell 'em I'm here . . . only don't tell nobody else."

"You runnin' from the law again?" Maude asked, without looking up from her carrots.

"You're a nosy ol' bitch. Just don't tell nobody 'cept for Clyde or Sloan that you seen me."

Maude chuckled. "If I was to tell the law 'bout every man with a price on his head who boards with me, I'd be a rich woman. Get upstairs an' put your stuff away. You could damn sure use a bath, Carl. For a minute there I thought some of these carrots was rotten. But it was you I was smellin'. Two buckets of hot water costs a nickle more . . . includes the price of soap an' a towel."

"I don't need no damn bath, woman. Fix me a plate of them beans."

He went into a darkened hallway and climbed familiar steps to the top floor. He'd stayed at Maude's plenty of times in the past, like dozens of men on the run. Maude Day was a grouchy old woman, but she could be trusted. She ran a "safe house" that was well known from Texas to the backwoods of western Tennessee, if you knew who to ask.

Carl shucked his duster and hung it on a peg, taking his last clean shirt from his war bag. It *had* been weeks since he had a hot bath, or anything other than hard ground to sleep on.

Heading back down to the kitchen, he wondered what kind of job Sloan wanted to tell him about. Of all the gunmen he'd known in his lifetime, including Ben Thompson, none was any faster or any deadlier with a pistol than Sloan Wilson. He'd teamed up with Sloan a number of times.

Clyde Wall, on the other hand, didn't have the stomach for the outlaw trade. He was short on nerve. Sloan and Clyde didn't seem a likely pair to be involved in anything dangerous.

"Fix me that damned hot water," Carl said to

Maude when he came into the kitchen. "But just so's you'll know, it ain't me stinkin'. It's this goddamn fleabag boardin' house that's got the bad smell."

Chapter 19

The Cottage was a small yet opulent place, with glass doors and mirrors on every wall. Pauline sat across from Leo while a waitress took their order for pork ribs in red wine sauce, sweet potatoes baked with brown sugar, and collard greens cooked in a mixture of vinegar and other seasonings. Pauline recommended the dishes as a departure from the town's staple offerings: beef in any number of cuts and descriptions, with fried or mashed potatoes. The café sat on the north end of Texas Street, not far from the Alamo Saloon.

Their soft-spoken young waitress departed for the kitchen, then Pauline continued her discussion of the short history of Abilene, a topic she'd begun while they sat sipping brandy in the surrey on a starlit hilltop above the city. Leo had listened attentively, noticing Pauline snuggle a bit closer to him in the chill night air . . . until she caught herself and asked to be taken to dinner, sliding away from him on the buggy seat with the comforter over her lap.

"It is taken from the Bible, I've been told. It means 'city of the prairie' in Hebrew, I believe." She drank from a crystal goblet filled with imported sherry, making an obvious effort not to stare at Leo too often.

"You are remarkably well versed in the history having to do with this region," Leo observed. "It must have required quite a bit of study on your part."

She touched her linen napkin to her lips. "Not really. I am only repeating what others have said about the origins of Abilene. As a city, it hasn't existed long, only a few years. Its only reason for existence is to service the beef industry back East. Truthfully, I find this a terrible place to live. There is no culture, no library, no interest in literature. Most of the men and women who come here, either to stay or as seasonal visitors, can scarcely read.

"It has, as a town, several faces, I suppose. The business district is almost entirely devoted to the wants and needs of cattle drovers. It has two railroads, including the Union Pacific and the Kansas and Pacific. A dentist advertises 'almost painless tooth extraction' on the same street where harness repair and a blacksmith's shop sit side-by-side. Across the road I saw a sign touting the virtues of Thistleberry Tonic for stomach ailments and headache remedy 'for those who consume too much strong drink.' Next door is a saloon peddling distilled spirits. Where there is a vice, there is also a cure, it would seem. And then one must consider the Devil's Addition, where virtually any form of pleasure sought by a drover is sold."

Pauline smiled. "The sin district. Dad calls it the place where money and whiskey flow like water downhill, and youth and beauty and womanhood are wrecked and damned in Abilene's valley of perdition. He says the women are known as soiled doves, or nymphs *du* prairie, calico queens or painted cats. He won't go down there, although my brother Jimmy goes quite often when Dad is otherwise occupied. He won't admit it, but I suspect he consorts with the district's soiled doves, and he seems fascinated by the seedy characters who frequent the saloons. Gunfighters in particular."

Leo enjoyed listening to the lilting quality of Pauline's voice. "Your brother may be headed down a dangerous course," he told her. "He fancies himself a gunman, despite the fact he has not been tested. I hope he seeks another interest before he goes too far."

She looked down at her hands. "I know. He

and Dad don't get along. Jimmy isn't interested in the cattle business. He's drawn into associations with bad men, professional gunmen and the like. I've tried talking to him about it. He won't listen to me and I worry about him."

"A beautiful lady like you shouldn't worry."

Her cheeks darkened. "Do you really think I'm pretty, Dr. LeMat?"

"Please call me Leo. And my answer is yes."

"You embarrass me. I don't think I'm all that pretty when I see myself in a mirror."

He fingered his glass of sherry. "I have had occasion to travel rather extensively, Pauline. I've seen women of every description during my travels, and I can assure you that you are among the most beautiful women I've ever seen."

Her blush deepened and she found she couldn't look at him. "Please stop. I'm grateful that you find me attractive. For reasons I can't explain, hearing you say it makes me a bit uncomfortable now."

"I apologize. I have no wish to cause you distress. I was merely making an observation."

Pauline giggled, perhaps due to the sherry. "You make me feel like a schoolgirl. Your manners are so polished, and you have a way with words."

"I am only describing what I see."

She took another sip from her goblet. "Let's talk about something else, if you don't mind."

"I do not mind at all. Tell me about you— what you want from life, where you're from and where you wish to go. What you'd like to do if you had every opportunity."

Her hazel eyes sparkled. "I would dearly love to attend the opera in New York or San Francisco. I have seen tintypes of their beautiful opera houses, the elaborate costumes, and music is one of my passions."

"A passion?"

"Unfortunately, it is a passion I cannot satisfy where my father makes his living. Music in Abilene does not exist, unless you consider a barroom fiddler or a piano player a musician. We moved here from Chicago, where symphony orchestras play almost every weekend. I do miss that so very much. I love fine music and there is none to be found here."

He grinned, remembering his walk into the Devil's Addition and the off-key piano player. "How well I know," he said. "Only this very afternoon I heard the worst attempt at piano playing on earth coming from the sin district, as you call it. The poor man must have ten thumbs."

Pauline frowned. "Why would you go to Deviltown?" she asked.

"To see a man by the name of Ben Thompson. He is also a shootist of considerable reputation, like Marshal Hickok. I intended to make his acquaintance. At some later date I may consider painting his portrait."

"What is it like to be a painter? I've wondered about it many times, how someone can have the skill to create a painting from a blank piece of canvas."

"I'd be hard-pressed to describe what goes on in my mind while I'm painting. I see small details, some only in my imagination. I paint from memory as well as what I have before me."

"How strange, and wonderful." She hesitated a moment. "I have a curiosity in regard to you, Leo. It may be a question you prefer not to answer."

"Ask me anything. I have few secrets."

Pauline seemed unsure where to begin. "The shooting on the train. You killed a man, and so did Jacques. I think it has been bothering my father, and I've been wondering about it too. You are a painter of portraits and a physician by profession, and yet you carry a gun. You shot one of the masked bandits when he tried to rob you. Being a doctor and an artist are compatible occupations, but Dad says your business card advertises that your gun is for hire, and that you kill people for money. Yet you don't seem the type."

He smiled and took out one of his cards, placing it on the tablecloth in front of her. "I'll try to explain. I studied medicine at my father's behest. My uncle is also a practitioner of the healing arts. I attended the university of Pennsylvania in order to receive my medical education. While I was there, I met one of this country's most famous portraitists, Mr. George Catlin. I've always had an interest in art. From the age of six or seven I began drawing charcoal sketches, but I lacked any professional training. By chance, and a stroke of luck, Mr. Catlin happened to see me sketching a young woman's face in a park close to the university. He stopped to examine my crude drawing. At the time I did not know who he was. When he introduced himself I was keenly embarrassed that he'd seen my poor rendition of the girl's face. Then he made a comment that would change the course of my life."

"Go on," Pauline said, a gentle look in her eyes.

"He told me I had a great talent, and furthermore, that I had an obligation to employ it to its full use. He gave me the address of his studio, inviting me to drop by at my convenience if I cared to master a few techniques."

"I'm sure you were flattered."

He nodded. "Almost beyond words. The famous portraitist, George Catlin, telling me I had artistic talent. It was my private dream come true."

"Did your father and uncle approve?"

"Not at all. My father was keenly disappointed and we seldom spoke or wrote to each other after that. But I knew I'd been granted a rare opportunity, to study under Catlin, and upon completion of my medical degree I continued to work closely with Mr. Catlin for well over a year."

Pauline frowned. "You still haven't explained the part about offering your services with a gun."

Leo drank the last of his sherry. "I confess I have a dark side. My uncle was granted a patent for a pistol called the LeMat, the very gun I carry now. There is a part of me that will not sit by idly when a bully with a gun tries to take advantage of peaceful people. In truth, I have a terrible temper when it comes to such matters. Over the years I discovered I was gifted, if you wish to call it that, with an uncommon dexterity when it comes to gunmanship. I can offer no better explanation. My reflexes are good, and I suppose the same critical eye I use to capture a subject on canvas with my oils provides me with good aim. I rarely ever miss. But in my own defense, let me say that I never employ my gun for illegal or nefarious purposes. I am capable of defending myself fairly well, as in the case of the foiled train robbery, and there have been times when I have put the same skill to use to bring down a wanted man, when the crime goes unpunished. And I will also confess that my temper causes me never to back down from an outright challenge. Peace-loving men are neither bullies nor antagonistic drunks who go looking for a fight. On the other hand, when someone causes me an affront or challenges me to a duel, I gladly oblige them."

"You *do* have a darker side, Leo. Even your face changes when you talk about guns and killing. Frankly, hearing you discuss it frightens me."

"You have nothing to fear from me, Pauline. I have inherited my mother's temper, it would seem, however I have learned to keep it under control . . . in most instances. An angry man with a gun makes mistakes. Often fatal mistakes. I enjoy life and my art far too much to risk ending my existence foolishly."

"My father is a good judge of character. He told me he is convinced you are a dangerous man. He only allowed me to go to dinner with you after I threatened to pack my valises and leave our house forever."

Leo couldn't help grinning. "A woman knows

how to get her way. I'm certain he only had your best interests in mind, but as you can see, I'm really not dangerous." He turned serious now. "While I am sorry your father feels that way about me, there is little I can do about it."

"For some reason, I find I'm beginning to trust you, Leo. You have been a perfect gentleman this evening."

"And I shall continue to be, if you will permit me to take you to dinner again sometime."

"Perhaps. But as soon as you've finished with your portrait of Marshal Hickok, you'll be leaving Abilene, won't you?"

He fixed her with a steady gaze. "For the right reasons, I might be persuaded to stay longer . . ."

Their food arrived, platters brimming with steaming ribs and sugar-laden sweet potatoes.

"It looks delicious," he said, turning to the waitress. "If you will, please bring us glasses of your best wine. Pork must be eaten with wine, as I'm sure you know. A good French merlot, if you have it."

"Of course, sir." The girl scurried off toward the kitchen.

Chapter 20

Sloan remained quiet all the way to the cabin, following Clyde through the darkness along a creek leading away from the Solomon River. It was a two-hour ride from Owen Bell's house to the old shack where the rest of the gang stayed holed up during the day. According to Clyde, the boss didn't like having his men ride to Abilene, where Marshal Hickok or Sheriff Jones might recognize them from wanted posters.

In a dense stand of oaks, they spotted lantern light beaming from cabin windows.

"Hold up while I give 'em the signal," Clyde said, reining his horse to a halt. "Wouldn't want the boys to start shootin' at us in the dark."

"Who else is here?" Sloan asked.

"Tully an' Jess. We don't hardly use no last names round here. No need." He cupped his hands around his mouth and gave a poor imitation of the call of an owl three times.

"I ain't all that fond of Mr. Bell, Clyde," Sloan said. "But I reckon the money's good enough so's I can tolerate him for a while."

"He pays good," Clyde remarked, as the door to the cabin opened. "Only he is kinda strange."

"I damn near killed his mulatto nigra," Sloan recalled. "If a man aims a gun at me, don't matter who he is or what color he happens to be, I'm gonna kill him if I can."

"That you, Clyde?" a squeaky voice asked when a shape came to the door frame.

"It's me!" he called back, touching a spur to his horse's ribs. Then he spoke to Sloan. "Moses Cade is Mr. Bell's personal bodyguard. Been with him for years. I figure he had orders to keep an eye on you, since you was a stranger."

"Wasn't his goddamn eyes worryin' me. That shotgun damn near got shoved up his ass sideways, when he kept on pointin' it at me."

"Mr. Bell's real careful 'bout most things. Now that he knows you, Moses won't do that no more."

They rode up to the shack. A skinny cowboy wearing two guns with his face shaded by a shapeless cowboy hat gave Clyde a wave, but kept his eyes on Sloan. Another man, bareheaded with a big balding spot atop his skull, lowered a Winchester rifle.

"Boys," Clyde began, "this here's Sloan.

Sloan, the short feller inside is Jess. This lanky gent who don't look like he eats too good is Tully."

Sloan nodded.

"You'll be Sloan Wilson," Tully said. "We ain't never met, but I've seen you round Fort Smith a time or two. You got one mean reputation with a gun, Mr. Wilson."

Clyde spoke up. "Sloan's gonna ride with us from now on. We just left the bossman's place an' Sloan's on the payroll now."

"Glad to have a man like you along," Tully said, as Sloan swung down from his roan to pull off his saddle and take down his gear.

Sloan offered no comment.

Clyde was stripping his own saddle off the bay. "We may have us another feller in a day or two, accordin' to Sloan. Man by the name of Carl Pickins is headed for Abilene. Him an' Sloan is friends."

"Can he shoot?" Jess asked.

Clyde provided the answer when Sloan made it clear he wasn't in a talkative mood. "He'll shoot damn near anything that walks or rides a horse. I've ridden with him. Don't get in his way if he starts shootin', 'cause you'll damn sure wind up shot full of holes if you do."

"That'll make five of us," Tully said. "It'll be

enough to take a train, what with Sloan now bein' on our side of things."

Clyde tossed his saddle in the dirt fork-first. "The boss said he got word the Friday night Union Pacific next week will have cow buyin' money on it, for when the herds come in. We'll hit it at the water stop, same as usual, unless Sloan's got a better idea."

"Knockin' it off the tracks makes more sense," Sloan said, carrying his saddle to a hitch rail to keep it off the ground. "They could be expectin' us at a water stop, if that's where you boys been hittin' 'em before. All we gotta do is cut down a tree and lay it over the tracks right after dark. The engineer won't see it till it's too late. A train is heavy . . . hard to stop with steam brakes in a short distance. We find the right bend in the tracks, it'll work."

Clyde chuckled. "Sloan's done a few trains before, boys, so we listen to him. Now we've got us a man with some railroad experience."

Tully and Jess laughed.

"Come in, Mr. Wilson," Tully said. "Moses jus' brung us a new batch of whiskey."

Sloan stopped in front of Tully, giving him a cold stare. "Don't ever call me by my last name again," he snapped. "I'd hate like hell to kill you over somethin' so small."

"Yessir. I mean, no sir. I won't call you Mr. Wilson no more."

Sloan walked into the shack, finding typical cowboy cots and a potbelly stove near a crude plank table and benches. He put his war bag down next to an empty bunk. Jess offered him a bottle of redeye.

He took a bubbling swallow and sleeved off his lips. "I'm gonna ride back to Abilene tonight, to see if Maude's heard anything from Carl."

"The boss won't like it, Sloan," Clyde warned. "He's done told you he don't want none of us hangin' around town."

"I don't give a damn what he told us, Clyde. If we're gonna pull a train robbery, we'll need another man who knows how it's done."

"We ain't done all that bad ourselves," Jess protested, a puzzled look clouding his expression.

Sloan gave him back the jug. "It damn sure don't sound like it to me," he said tonelessly. "You lost two men the last time, an' didn't get away with a cent."

"But it was that fancy-suited feller an' the little bastard wearin' the sailor's cap," Clyde argued. "We had that train almost robbed till them two jumped in."

"Try spendin' all that money you took from

the safe," Sloan replied. "See how much whiskey you can buy with it."

"Just shut up, Clyde," Tully said from a corner of the room. "Mr.— Sloan knows what he's doin', that's for damn sure."

Chapter 21

Leo escorted Pauline out of the Cottage, holding the door open for her, blissfully content after their delicious meal, prepared with skill equal to that of Jacques. But of far more importance, their conversation had been spirited and pleasant. He found the young woman most entertaining, and a delight to be with.

He took her arm to walk her to the rented surrey where the chestnut buggy horse stood quietly, its head lowered, its snaffle bridle bit fastened to a harness weight to keep the animal from wandering off.

"Thank you again for dinner, Leo," she said, coming to the single carriage step, where he assisted her onto the seat.

"The pleasure was entirely and distinctly mine," he told her. "I cannot remember when I've enjoyed an evening more. The food was marvelous, and your recommendation of the pork ribs proved to be the best choice. Beyond that, who would expect to find a delicate chocolate mousse in the middle of a prairie? I was pleasantly surprised."

He had walked around to the front of the surrey to unhitch the harness flatiron, when a movement along the boardwalks fronting Texas Street caught his eye.

"Ah, it's Sheriff Jones," he said, dropping the weight onto the surrey's floorboard.

"Dr. LeMat! I need a word with you!"

The tone of the sheriff's voice alerted him to difficulties, yet Leo could not imagine what had brought Roy Jones looking for him in this part of town at night.

"Of course, Sheriff," he answered, standing next to a front buggy wheel.

Sheriff Jones and a young slope-shouldered deputy carrying a shotgun walked over. The look on the sheriff's face confirmed Leo's first guess. Something was definitely amiss, yet he wondered what it might have to do with him.

Jones saw Pauline sitting in the surrey seat and tipped his hat to her. "Evenin', Miss Matlock. Sorry to disturb you, but I need to talk to the doctor in private."

Leo was more curious than ever now. "Whatever you have to say to me can be said in front of the lady."

Jones swallowed. "Suit yourself, Doc. I got a wire from U.S. Marshal Heck Thomas in Fort Smith regardin' you and them Gold Knights. Just so happens that Miss Matlock's father came by my office right afterwards. He wanted to know about you, about who you was. I told him what was in the wire, an' he informed me where you'd taken his daughter for supper. That's how I found you so easy."

Leo heard Pauline sigh impatiently. "Go on, Sheriff. What did Marshal Thomas have to say?" he asked.

"First off, he said Judge Parker told him them Knights wasn't no more. Broke up after the war. Then he warned me 'bout you."

"About me? I think I've only met Heck Thomas once, down in Texas some years ago."

"He mentioned that. Said you was a stone-cold killer. A bounty hunter of the worst kind. He seen you kill two men himself a few years back in San Antone."

Leo shrugged. "It's possible, I suppose, but if you'll wire Captain Lee Dobbs of the Texas Rangers' post in Bexar County, I assure you you'll find that no charges have ever been filed against me for a murder, or any other crime."

"He didn't say you was no criminal. Said you was a paid killer, an' to keep an eye on you. He wondered what you was doin' in Abilene. I told him that cock an' bull story you told me, about bein' here to paint Hickok. I never did believe that tale."

Leo struggled to control his swelling anger, most especially in front of the woman. "It is no 'cock and bull story,' as you put it, that I came to Abilene to paint Marshal Hickok's portrait. If you have doubts, speak with the marshal about our appointment at my hotel tomorrow afternoon at one. As to the part about keeping an eye on me, you are welcome to do so. However, I resent any implication that I am a hired murderer or a wanton killer. It offends me."

Jones straightened his shoulders. "Well, sir, you can just keep on bein' offended. I got it straight from the U.S. Marshal's office that you was a bounty hunter. I reckon it's up to Hickok if you do your killin' inside the city limits, but if you want some advice, I'd hook that fancy railroad car to the next train out of town before you do any killin' here."

Pauline's presence prevented him from a more direct reply to the sheriff's unwanted advice. Leo kept his voice calm. "I mean to stay until I'm finished with my portrait of the marshal. Unless I've broken some law for which you intend to arrest me tonight, then we'll be on our way."

Sheriff Jones appeared to shrink in front of

Leo's chilly response. "Suit yourself, LeMat. I reckon if you break any city ordinances, it'll be up to Bill to see to it that you get the right punishment. Just wanted you to know that I know who you are, an' what you do for a livin'."

Leo clamped his teeth. "As long as what I do for a living is within the law, Sheriff, it is none of your concern. Now if you'll excuse us, I'm driving Miss Matlock home."

Leo was seething inside, trying not to let it show for Pauline's sake, as he drove the surrey down dark streets toward her father's house.

She spoke for the first time since they left the front of the Cottage. "I can't imagine that you are a professional killer, Leo."

"I am sorry this happened to spoil our evening, Pauline. I cannot explain it. I am not a bounty hunter, as the telegram from Fort Smith alleged."

"I believe you," she answered softly, when the surrey pulled up to her house. "Good night, Leo. It might be best, since my father will certainly be influenced by what Sheriff Jones told him, that you not walk me to the door."

"I understand," he said. "I'll wait out here until you are safely inside before I drive away." He swung down quickly to help her out of the seat.

She surprised him when she stood on her tip-toes to give him a light kiss on the lips. "I hope to see you again," she whispered, wheeling away to hurry up the front porch steps.

Chapter 22

He sat in his room, contemplating the faint charcoal lines on his canvas by the pale light thrown by three lanterns, sipping brandy until the hour passed midnight. A cool breeze lifted the curtains in lazy swirls away from open windows. Off to the east, a banjo player in the Devil's Addition battled a piano and a drum from another establishment, a cacophonous duel between strings and keys and drumsticks so offensive to the ear, that even listening to howling alley cats would have been more soothing.

Since returning the rented surrey and retiring to his room, Leo found himself in a strange, pensive mood. The words spoken by Sheriff Jones in Pauline's presence still echoed through his memory. He wished now he'd agreed to hold their conversation in private, although Pauline's father had already been told what Marshal Heck Thomas had wired to the sheriff. It was all a black lie, he thought, a distorted version of events having to do with a pair of San Antonio shootings. Both wanted by the law, Doyle Allison and Billy Roberts had such fearsome reputations that the Bexar County sheriff avoided confronting them while they were in town. Leo had been asked by a friend, the owner of the Cactus Cantina on Presa Street, to help him rid his establishment of their bullying tactics. Roberts and Allison were driving away all his better customers. Leo had been reluctant to oblige his friend, entering a fight that wasn't his, but he went to the Cactus and ordered both men to leave. Allison got surly and went for his gun in front of the cantina.

"Such is the grist for undeserved reputations," Leo sighed, sipping the last of his Martel. There had been dozens of witnesses to the Allison killing, exonerating Leo from any murder charges.

Sad, he believed, that lovely Pauline Matlock now thought of him as a professional killer, even though she denied it. Her father would be all too willing to believe Heck Thomas's version. From what Leo knew about Thomas, in his early years he was no candidate for sainthood himself, until Judge Isaac Parker, the so-called "Hanging Judge," offered him a marshal's badge.

The sudden rattle of gunfire in the district took Leo from his recollections of San Antonio and dinner with Pauline. He got up and walked to a window as the shooting ended. Faint laughter followed the gunshots, marking the incident as a celebration rather than an occasion for violence.

Jacques was yet to return, proof of his success deflowering the Cherokee girl somewhere in Abilene. The thought made Leo smile. Jacques was no beginner in the art of seduction, a fact Anatoka would, no doubt, discover tonight.

Though the hour was late, Leo felt a nudge of curiosity. What would his subject, Bill Hickok, be like under the heavy influence of alcohol? It might be well worth the trip to wander down to the Bull's Head, merely as an observer of Hickok's behavior while in his true element. Watching his actions could be a help finding the inner being Leo hoped to portray on canvas.

Promising himself to avoid trouble at all costs, he nonetheless buckled on his shoulder holster, a precaution against any unforeseen confrontations. He slipped into his coat and covered his face with the brim of his black Stetson, before putting out the lanterns and locking the door behind him. By approaching the sin district from the rear, he could move about unnoticed in the dark and, by chance, get a look at Hickok without the marshal being aware.

The stench of urine from the open sewer ditches behind rows of saloons assailed Leo's nostrils. Despite it being early in the year for the arrival of big cattle herds, the district was full of celebrating cowboys. An occasional gunshot popped from somewhere on the streets now and then, and even more assaults upon music were being attempted in a number of drinking parlors. Leo's accomplished ear easily recognized a wailing guitar with a missing string, a piano badly in need of tuning, and a banjo and drummer who hurried their faltering Dixie beat, attempting to keep up with the rousing cheers from listeners certain to be Texans.

Leo found the rear of the Bull's Head and made his way up an opening between buildings, pausing at a side window sheltered by deep shadows in order to watch what was taking place inside. The smoky room was half-empty, and Marshal Hickok was easy to spot at a corner table with a bottle of wine before him, playing poker in the company of four cowboys. Leo recognized one of the players after a closer look. Young James Matlock, his hat pushed back on his head, held a fistful of cards and wore a gun tied low on his leg. Pauline had been right to suppose her brother enjoyed rough company in the district.

Ben Thompson sat at another card table with a cigar held loose between his teeth, dealing a round of five-card stud. Most of the money on the table was piled in front of him.

Casey, the bartender who had only today committed murder over a case of the pox, hurried to refill beer mugs and shotglasses for a pair of dewy-eyed waitresses a few years past their prime, dressed in satin corsets and silk stockings, their hair done up in ribbons. Leo found the Bull's Head a poor imitation of a fine gaming house in New Orleans or San Antonio, until he considered its location and clientele. The place was probably suited for a Kansas cow town.

He studied Hickok's movements, thankful for the opportunity to do so without the marshal's notice. But in spite of the loud voices and other distractions, Hickok kept a wary eye on the front doors quite often. And his back was to the wall, Leo noticed, away from any windows.

A moment later the marshal spoke to Jimmy Matlock. Leo was too far away to hear what he said. Hickok put down his cards and reached for a pistol, demonstrating his road agent's spin before returning the Colt to its holster. Jimmy's

eyes were riveted on Hickok, then he grinned
and shook his head.

Even half-drunk, he's good . . . and careful, Leo
thought. Wild Bill still seemed to have good in-
stincts for survival, and his eyes appeared to be
quite clear, watchful, untouched by the effects
of alcohol.

Later, Leo walked into the street to find the
best bottle of sour mash he could purchase,
avoiding groups of cowhands idling on saloon
porches due to the obvious difference in his
dress. He intended to return to the Bull's Head
as closing time neared for a final examination
of Hickok's behavior, following a full night of
drinking. It was a high price to pay, observing
his subject in the midst of trenches filled with
urine, but worth it, in Leo's estimation. George
Catlin insisted a man's pose for a portrait
showed only his public image, the one he
wanted to project. The keener powers of an artist's observation, he had always said, came into
play when a subject was unaware of being
watched.

The crowd inside the Bull's Head began to
thin as the hour approached two in the morning.
Leo was tired of watching Hickok and he felt
he'd seen enough to satisfy his curiosity. Ben

Thompson had left earlier by the swinging doors, in the company of a young woman.

Leo had turned away from the window to walk softly between the buildings, when a shadowy figure coming toward the back door of the Bull's Head froze him in his tracks.

A corpulent man in a battered derby hat made his way to the rear of the saloon, opening a sawed-off shotgun to check its loads, moving on the balls of his feet. He wore a gun belt, and it was all too clear he meant to enter the saloon, intent upon an act of violence, although he swayed a bit drunkenly while he inspected his shotgun before snapping the barrels back in place.

Does he mean to kill Hickok? Leo wondered, remaining motionless to keep from being noticed. *I can't allow it. My portrait is not yet begun.*

When the gunman climbed a set of wooden steps to enter from the rear, Leo pulled his revolver. If this stranger in the derby intended to seek some sort of revenge against the marshal, Leo meant to halt it.

"Your name's Casey, ain't it?" The stranger's gun was not aimed directly at Hickok, albeit he kept swinging it back and forth to cover the entire room.

The bartender nodded once, backing away,

his hands raised high above his head. "I'm Casey. What do you want with me?"

"You killed a friend of mine today, an unarmed woman who never done you no harm. Kate Sparks was her name. They called her Flat Nose Kate." He turned his gun toward Hickok's table, where Jimmy Matlock was still seated. "You stay outta this, Bill. Got nothin' to do with you. It's between me an' this bartendin' son of a bitch. He's gonna get what's comin' to him, so don't try an' stop me!"

Hickok's hands rested on the tabletop, one fist filled with playing cards. "I know you," Hickok said. "Carl. Carl Pickins. Don't do it, Carl. Ben ain't gonna take it kindly if you kill his barkeep."

"He killed Kate, Bill. Wasn't no call for it, either."

"She . . . gave me . . . the Pox," Casey stammered, his hands still high. "I'm gonna die from it."

"You're gonna die right now, asshole, for killin' Kate like you done." Jimmy Matlock pushed back his chair and stood up, squaring himself in front of Pickins. "I ain't gonna let you shoot him down, mister!" he cried, tensing as if he meant to reach for his pistol.

"Sit back down, son," Hickok said quietly, "or

you're gonna get yourself killed. Carl Pickens ain't nobody to try your luck with."

Jimmy glanced over his shoulder. "I can take him, Marshal Hickok," he protested.

"Sit down, boy!" Carl demanded. "You ain't got no part in this."

Jimmy's face lost some of its color as he sat back down in his chair. Carl swung his shotgun back on Casey, but with an eye on Hickok. "Kiss your ass good-bye, barman. You ain't gonna kill no lady friend of mine without payin' for it. I don't give a damn what Ben Thompson's gonna think."

Leo had listened to enough, standing in the shadows of a storeroom at the back of the building. Walking soundlessly, he crept up behind Carl Pickins and placed the barrel of his LeMat against the base of his skull. "Be very still, my friend," he said, barely above a whisper. "One move, one *twitch*, and I'll make what few brains you have a part of this ceiling. Lower the shotgun and do it very slowly. I beg you not to test my resolve in this matter, Mr. Pickins, for I will kill you as surely as you stand here." He cocked his pistol, and the sound was like a clap of thunder in the silence of the Bull's Head.

Pickins remained motionless, his shotgun aimed at Casey.

"I know what you're thinking," Leo continued, his voice now hoarse, grating, filled with menace. "You're wondering if you're fast enough to wheel around before I pull this trigger. Let me assure you that you'll be much too slow. There will be a tunnel through your head before you make a quarter turn . . . a very large tunnel. You won't hear or feel a thing. It will be as if the lights went out. No pain, no suffering, simply an immediate death. You'll be with your friend Kate."

Something in Leo's warning was enough to convince Pickins to toss down his scattergun. It landed near his boots with a thud.

"A very wise choice, Mr. Pickins," Leo said. "Now I'll take your pistol, and the bellygun you carry under your shirt. I'm not all that concerned about the knife in your boot, or the butt of the derringer I see; however, I feel I must warn you that one move toward another weapon will have the same result I promised you before. Have you ever seen bloody brain tissue hanging from a ceiling? It's an awful mess to clean up."

Marshal Hickok came out of his chair with a pistol in each fist. "I'll take him from here, Doc. Carl's gonna be a guest at my steel hotel. We have nice, comfortable beds and I hear the food is better'n most, although I won't eat it. Sometimes my prisoners get the bellyache." He walked over to the bar and stepped behind it until his gun muzzles were against Carl's belly. "Good to see you again, Carl," he added, a mock grin creasing his cheeks. He holstered one revolver and jerked Pickins's pistol free, resting it on the bar.

"Two more, Marshal," Leo said. "The little bulge under his shirt is probably a thirty-two. You'll find a knife and a derringer in his boot tops." Very slowly, he lowered the hammer on his LeMat and took a step backward.

"Nice work, Doc," Hickok said, removing Pickins's bellygun, then the daggerlike Arkansas toothpick and the derringer. "I didn't expect to see you in this end of town, but I'm glad you came. It saved me from having to kill a man."

Leo let the marshal's remark pass. "I'm only doing my civic duty as a visitor to your fair city, Marshal Hickok. I'm quite sure you could have handled the situation alone. I merely happened to be passing by when I saw this fellow coming through the back door with a gun."

Casey had lowered his palms. "I'm mighty grateful to you, Doc. Let me pour you a coupla drinks on the house."

He tucked his pistol inside his coat. "It's late, but I thank you anyway." Remembering the Matlock boy, he looked across the room. "This fellow would've killed you, James. He had a shotgun leveled on you. There's a lesson to be learned from tonight's episode: Never challenge a man to a duel if he already has his weapon aimed in your direction. Even the best of gunmen understand discretion over valor when they stand no chance of winning."

Leo tipped his hat to the marshal. "Have a pleasant evening, Marshal Hickok. I'm looking forward to our appointment at one o'clock."

Leo left as he'd come in, by the rear door, striding across the slop made by open sewers, to reach his hotel room. For a moment or two he'd been sure Carl Pickins would make his play, and some inner part of Leo's nature felt inexplicably disappointed when things ended so peacefully.

Chapter 23

As Leo was walking behind the rows of saloons, he heard the thunder of running horses' hooves coming hard and fast down Texas Street.

Someone's in a hell of a hurry, he thought.

Peering through the darkness between two buildings, he saw a man and a woman galloping toward the Bull's Head. Even in the poor light coming from the front windows of saloons, he recognized the woman at once—it was Pauline, dressed in a man's garb. And her father rode alongside her.

"What would bring them to this part of town?" Leo muttered, making his way back toward the Bull's Head to see what had brought them out at this hour.

Pauline and John reined in at the saloon. Pauline was dressed in denims and a man's work shirt. John Matlock was wearing a gun belt. A Winchester rifle was booted to his saddle.

They rushed through the doors into the Bull's Head just before Leo caught up with them.

"Marshal Hickok!" John shouted. "You've gotta help us. A night rider for the Aller outfit just rode into town to say he spotted those damn Ghost Riders headed for the railroad water stop east of town. My money's on that train . . . money I need to buy a herd comin' in from Texas."

Hickok had Carl Pickins in wrist irons. "It's out of my jurisdiction, John. How come you didn't tell the county sheriff about it?"

"We tried," Pauline cried, without realizing that Leo was standing behind her. "He said he had the gout and couldn't put his boots on. He insisted there was nothing he could do."

"The yellow bastard," John growled. "I was hoping you'd help us, Marshal Hickok." He glared at Jimmy. "Get up from that damn card game son, and get mounted."

Jimmy came quickly to his feet. "At last I'm gonna get to do some shootin'," he said eagerly.

Leo spoke softly, surprising both Pauline and John with his presence. "Did this night rider say how many Ghost Riders he saw headed for the train?"

John answered. "Said there was at least seven. Maybe one or two more. He lit out for town to tell me an' the sheriff about it soon as he saw 'em. A helluva lot of good it did to tell Roy Jones." Matlock frowned. "That fancy business card of yours says your gun is for hire. I'll pay you a fair price to ride to that train with me an' Jimmy . . . since I can't get any help from the law," he added, glaring at Hickok. "We're gonna need every gun we can get."

Leo nodded. "It won't be necessary to pay me, Mr. Matlock. I'll help you simply out of my acquaintance with your daughter. I'll get my rifle and rent a horse from the livery." Then he gave Hickok an amused look. "I would think you'd enjoy a little gunplay tonight, Marshal. It's good for the circulation. Some say it's invigorating, so long as you don't get any lead poisoning from it."

Hickok seemed undecided. He sighed, and then he said, "What the hell. I'll toss Mr. Pickins in jail and saddle my gray. I'll get Ben Thompson out of that whore's crib so he can ride along. He likes a good fight as well as any man I ever knew."

Jimmy raced out the batwings to look for his horse. John took Pauline by the arm and said, "Go home, honey. You shouldn't be in this part of town in the first place."

"Please be careful, Dad," she said as John escorted her out the doors.

Hickok pushed Carl Pickins outside with the

muzzle of a pistol. He spoke to Leo and John as he swung his prisoner toward the center of town. "I'll fetch my horse and rouse Ben. We'll meet in front of my office."

Leo found the piebald pinto gelding to his liking, with an easy rein and long strides at a gallop. They rode five abreast at a steady lope along the eastbound rails, making as much time as they could in the dark.

Ben Thompson carried a shotgun cradled against his thigh, talking to Hickok while they rode. "Sure hope we catch up to 'em in time, Bill. That water stop ain't but a few more miles an' I don't hear no shootin'."

"I sure hope I get the chance to kill a few," Jimmy said, spurring his chestnut a little harder.

"Shut up, son," John scolded. "A shootin' match ain't no damn picnic. You'd better hope you ain't the one who gets a slug in his gut."

Leo remained silent, listening to the banter, his Winchester loaded, as was his LeMat. He thought about his companions in the fight that might lie ahead. Hickok was no doubt a good marksman, but what would he be like when he was half-drunk?

John Matlock was a cattle buyer and probably knew little or nothing about a gun. Jimmy Matlock was too green to be of any help.

Ben Thompson, on the other hand, would likely be the most valuable. He had a cold, confident air about him and his reputation down in Texas as a deadly killer was well deserved.

Leo decided the odds would have been more to his liking if Jacques had been along, but the little Cajun was off somewhere in Abilene attempting to deflower the young Indian maiden and there hadn't been time to look for him.

"Ain't far now," John said. "Maybe a couple more miles, if I remember right."

"I can't hardly wait to start killin' ghosts," Jimmy said, jerking his pistol free of its holster as his horse galloped over rough flint ground.

"Shut up, boy," John snapped again, "an' put that damn gun away until it comes time to use it. Hell, you're liable to shoot one of us before we get there."

Jimmy hunkered down inside his shirt collar after the scolding, but he did as he was told and put his pistol away.

Leo felt vaguely uneasy, having a green kid like Jimmy along who had no idea what death was about. It was no small thing to take from a man all he is and all he ever will be, having no understanding of the finality of it. And if the boy went on a wild shooting spree, he could easily fulfill his father's grim prophecy and kill the wrong man with a stray bullet. Leo knew all too well what a dreadful sight it was to look into a man's eyes as his life drained out of him . . . to know that you were the one who had turned him into a lifeless pile of flesh and bones. Even Leo's dark side recoiled at those moments, an odd contradiction he'd lived with since he killed his first man in a duel. But there were times when, for the sake of honor or to help a friend, killing became necessary. Leo often questioned whether it was good fortune or misfortune that he happened to have a gift for it.

His thoughts were interrupted by the distant rattle of guns from the east.

"Maybe we got here in the nick of time!" Thompson shouted, urging more speed from his horse.

They crossed a barren hilltop and saw the halted train at the water tower. The muzzle flashes of popping guns were easy to see in the dark.

"I see 'em! Jimmy shouted, jerking out his pistol again as the five riders closed the distance on the train.

"I count six!" Thompson bellowed. "There, by the baggage car!"

"Yonder's two more!" John Matlock cried.

Leo drew his Winchester and jacked a round into the firing chamber while the pounding of guns around the train grew louder. Horsemen in white robes and hoods were shooting at the baggage car. Sporadic bursts of answering fire came from small windows on either side of the closed baggage car door.

At a distance of two hundred yards, well beyond the range of a pistol, Jimmy Matlock started shooting, alerting the Ghost Riders to their presence.

Suddenly, the bandits' guns were turned on them. Stabbing fingers of yellow flame came at them, and the sizzle of hot lead whispered through the night air around them.

The damn young fool, Leo thought as he swung away from the others, waiting for the right target, the right range.

Now gun blasts came from all directions. Leo heard Thompson roar like a lion.

A white-cloaked rider appeared around the front of the locomotive, charging straight toward Leo. He jerked his LeMat free and took careful aim, cocking the center buckshot barrel for firing.

When he pulled the trigger, he felt the pistol's familiar kick and heard its mighty thunder. A bolt of white lightning pushed a hail of lead pellets into the night. The Ghost Rider twisted sideways in his saddle as a charge of grapeshot took his left arm off at the shoulder. A scream of pain echoed above the roar of guns as the outlaw was swept off his horse, landing disjointedly in a heap near the locomotive's cowcatcher.

Seconds later, Ben Thompson's shotgun exploded, toppling a bandit off the rump of his horse in a backwards somersault, his white robe blossoming red in light from the moon and stars. The outlaw shrieked before he hit the ground, skidding along on his back beside the rails.

The crack of a pistol downed Jimmy Matlock's horse, and he went flying over its head, tossing his pistol in the air before he fell. But as he tumbled toward the ground, a second shot made his body jerk in midair.

Leo took aim at the Ghost Rider who'd tagged Jimmy, but before he could squeeze off a shot, one of Bill Hickok's pistols barked. The robber slid out of his saddle and disappeared in the brush close to the rails.

Again, Thompson's shotgun blasted and an outlaw cried out in pain, slumping over the pommel of his saddle as he dropped the rifle he was carrying and wheeled his horse away from the train.

"Got the son of a bitch!" Thompson shouted.

The gunfire ended abruptly as four white-clad outlaws made a hasty retreat to the east.

"The sumbitches are gettin' away!" Hickok yelled.

"Let's ride the bastards down!" Thompson answered, spurring his mount after the robbers.

Leo jerked his pinto to a halt near the spot where Jimmy had fallen. John Matlock galloped up to the same spot and jumped from the saddle before Leo could dismount.

"Jimmy! Jimmy," John cried, kneeling in the brush. "How bad are you hit?"

Leo bent over Jimmy's prone form, discovering a superficial gash in the boy's neck that was leaking a considerable amount of blood.

"He'll be okay, Mr. Matlock," Leo said. "I'll get this bleeding stopped and we'll get him back to town. It's just a flesh wound."

"Thank God for that," John whispered, touching Jimmy's shoulder. "Maybe now my son's learned a lesson about a gunfight. I hope the hell he has."

Jimmy groaned, only half-conscious from his fall, then his eyes fluttered open. "What . . . happened?" he asked in a weak voice.

"You damn near got killed," his father replied as Leo took off his coat to make a bandage out of his shirtsleeve.

Off in the distance they heard Thompson's shotgun roar, and the crack of a pistol. Then all was quiet.

John stood up and glanced at the train. "There's one big consolation. They didn't break into the baggage car, so my money's safe." He looked down at Leo while he was tearing off his shirtsleeve. "I owe you a big one, Doc. Hickok an' Ben wouldn't have lifted a finger to help me if you hadn't goaded 'em into it. I sure as hell had the wrong opinion of you."

Right now, Leo didn't want any gratitude. Two members of the train crew came cautiously toward them.

Leo spoke to John. "Find one of those outlaws' horses and we'll get Jimmy back to Abilene so I can properly clean and dress his wound."

"Sure thing, Doc. And by the way, you're one hell of a shot with that strange-lookin' gun you carry. I saw it when you blew his arm plumb off. That's one hell of a shootin' iron."

Thompson and Hickok caught up to them as they rode slowly back toward Abilene holding a whimpering Jimmy Matlock in the bloodstained saddle of a bay horse.

"The rest of the bastards got away," Thompson complained bitterly. "Just when I was in a real good killin' mood. They split up an' we lost 'em in the dark."

Hickok spoke. "We killed three of them, and

a fourth is badly wounded. The engineer promised they'd bring him into town in the caboose. Makes a man feel good now and then, to get out and spill some outlaw blood."

"Damn right it does," Thompson agreed as they came in sight of the lights of Abilene.

Leo said nothing, although he wondered about men who enjoyed hunting men, even desperados, as if they were killing wild game for sport.

Leo found no satisfaction in what he'd done tonight, beyond the knowledge that he'd helped Pauline's father save his investment money.

"Wish the hell I'd brought along a bottle of wine," Hickok said. "It would have added a perfect touch to the evening."

Thompson grunted. "A perfect touch woulda been killin' all the sorry bastards. Dumbest lookin' bunch of train robbers I ever run across, wearing them silly white robes. One thing's for damn sure. We proved they ain't real ghosts."

Chapter 24

Leo had the room ready for Hickok's visit. An overstuffed straight-backed chair was placed near a window to take best advantage of the sun, and a bottle of red wine was sitting nearby on a table.

His easel was set up and he'd completed his charcoal sketch of Hickok's face and shoulders on the white background he'd painted on the canvas. All he had to do now was shade in the rest of his facial features. The lawman's eyes would be the most difficult, and Leo wondered if he'd be able to show the ferocity and the fierce glint in them.

Jacques was still asleep, having come in just prior to dawn. Leo was sure that he would have some exciting tales to tell of his adventures with Anatoka the night before.

Leo answered a knock on the door, and found Marshal Hickok in the hallway. He noticed

Hickok showed no obvious signs of the late night gun battle or the prodigious amount of wine he'd drunk. Evidently he was used to both.

"Good morning, Mr. Hickok," Leo said as he showed him to the chair by the window.

"Morning, Doc," Hickok said, reaching for his hat.

"No, please keep the hat on," Leo said. He placed Hickok in the chair, seated to the right, and tilted his hat back a bit to avoid casting a shadow on his face.

"Is it okay if I talk, or do I have to just sit here like a stone?" Hickok asked.

"Talk, by all means," Leo said. "As long as you keep the same relative position, you may talk or drink while I paint."

Leo rolled his sleeves up, stepped behind his easel and began to mix colors on his palette to get the perfect shades for Hickok's skin tones. He planned to leave the marshal's eyes for last, when every other feature and detail satisfied him.

"Helluva thing you did last night," Hickok said, already pouring himself a full glass of wine, then draining half of it in one long swallow.

"What do you mean?"

"Bracing Pickins like you did. Carl's one of the meanest bastards I've ever run across, except for John Wesley Hardin, of course. That Hardin boy ain't just mean . . . he's plumb out of his goddamn head! Then there was the way you took on them Ghost Riders. You're a good shot."

"Mr. Pickins didn't impress me as being all that dangerous," Leo said, continuing to paint as he talked. "Those outlaws didn't show much backbone either."

"I know Carl don't look all that bad, but he's been known to kill a man for no reason at all. He goes plumb crazy sometimes, and when he does, there ain't no stopping him short of putting him in a grave. Like you say, wasn't much to those ghosts, though."

"Pickins appeared drunk to me, and I felt some responsibility for the barkeeper's life."

Hickok scowled. "How's that? You ain't making much sense."

"I'm the one who told Casey he would die from the Pox, and that's the reason Casey shot Kate, Pickins's lady friend."

"It's the truth, ain't it?"

"I'm afraid it is. There is no cure for the Pox."

"Then you ain't got no responsibility. All you did was tell him what was gonna happen to him."

"What will happen to Pickins?"

Hickok looked surprised. "Why, nothing. Fact is, I already let him outta jail this morning."

"After threatening you with a shotgun?"

Hickok grinned. "Hell, he didn't threaten me, he was aiming it at Casey for the most part. That ain't a crime, unless he'd pulled the trigger. And like you say, he was drunk at the time."

"It still seems to me that he should spend some time in jail for threatening to kill a man."

"I could've taken him any time I wanted to. Hell, he took his eyes off me too many times. Besides, you had your gun at the back of his head. I figured you'd be the one to kill him."

Leo wondered how much of what Hickok said was merely boast.

"Course, I'll admit I was a bit . . . nervous about it, him having that scattergun already cocked."

"Most any sensible man would be, unless he was behind him."

"Truth is, as I sat there, wonderin' who was gonna blink first, I got to thinking about what you said the other day."

"About what, Marshal?"

"About how you was always a little scared before a gunfight, how it really didn't matter none so long as you owned up to it and did what you had to do." Hickok refilled his glass. "Matter of fact, I been doing a lot more thinking lately about dying than I ever did when I was younger."

Leo nodded. "The young always believe they are immortal. Their own death is unthinkable to them."

"Yeah. Hell, when I was riding scout and fighting Injuns and cattle thieves, I did things that were plumb crazy. Now that I'm a mite older and wiser—and maybe even a fraction slower—I catch myself wondering if the next drunk cowpoke who comes through a door might have a bullet in his gun with my name on it."

"A natural fear in your profession, Marshal."

Hickok shook his head, staring at his now empty wineglass. "That's the thing about getting older. Trying to live up to what's expected of you gets to be a chore. Sometimes when I do something, I wonder if I'm being Wild Bill, or just plain Bill Hickok. You know what I mean, Doc?"

"Sure, Bill. It's a common enough thing, to try to do what we think other people expect from us."

Leo noticed that in spite of the wine, Hickok was beginning to fidget in his chair. He didn't want the marshal to come to dislike sitting for his portrait and decided to call it a day. He'd managed to give detail to his upper body and he had a good start on Hickok's face. Not bad for the first hour's work, Leo thought. He covered the portrait with a sheet and stepped from behind the easel.

"That's enough for today, Marshal."

"Thank God," Hickok said, coming quickly to his feet. "I was startin' to feel like I had ants in my britches."

"A lot of people feel that way when they sit for portraits," Leo said, smiling. He pointed to the picture of Angeline on a nearby wall. "When I painted that portrait of my daughter, I thought I'd have to tie her down to get her to sit still."

Hickok walked over to stand before the painting. "Right pretty girl" he said, a wistful expression on his face. "I ain't never had the time, or found the right woman, to start a family."

"There's plenty of time, isn't there? You're still young enough."

Hickok shook his head. "Out here, a man lives to be past forty, he's considered an old-timer. People grow up fast and die young."

Leo was brushing in the finishing touches on his morning's work when Jacques ambled out of his bedroom, stifling a yawn. His expression was one of contentment.

"I was about to call an undertaker to see if he needed to measure you for a coffin," Leo said, pouring Jacques a cup of coffee from the hotel kitchen.

Jacques took a swallow, then grimaced. "What is this?" he asked, holding his cup away from his face in an obvious effort to avoid the smell.

"That's coffee without chicory. Since you decided to sleep until midafternoon, I had to make do with what the chef downstairs could provide."

Jacques frowned. "Do not call that *bastard* who cooks in the hotel kitchen a chef. He is a murderer, a killer of otherwise good meat and vegetables. The only seasoning he's ever heard of is salt, and he uses it so liberally that any dish he prepares will be preserved until the end of the century."

Leo took a sip of his coffee and leaned back in his chair, crossing his legs. "I can tell from the expression you first had on your face that I don't need to ask how the evening with Anatoka went."

"No, you do not," Jacques smiled. "I cannot understand why settlers were so set against Indians. She was, in all ways, most delightful."

Leo held up his hand. "Please spare me the details of your violation of the Cherokee maiden. You took unfair advantage of her, I'm quite sure."

"From your surly attitude I need not ask about your evening with the delightful Mademoiselle Pauline?"

Leo smiled. "You are correct, *mon ami*. She

was delightful, and very proper. All I have to
show for the night was a quick kiss good night,
although I did discover an eating establishment
worthy of your attention."

"In this heathen wilderness? I doubt it,"
Jacques scoffed. He tried another sip of his coffee, then put the cup aside. "So *la 'tite chatte* was
immune to your charms, eh?"

"The little kitten, as you call her, was rather
put off by the unexpected arrival of County
Sheriff Roy Jones."

"And what did the sheriff have to say?"

"He received a wire from Marshal Heck
Thomas in Fort Smith stating that I was an unsavory character, not to be trusted with women
or children or small animals, or something to
that effect."

Jacques chuckled. "Whoever this Marshal
Thomas is, I feel compelled to congratulate him.
He has described you as well as any man ever
has; an unsavory character who defiles young
prairie flowers with absolutely no regrets or
feelings of remorse."

Leo's eyelids hooded in a show of sarcastic
anger. "And you are one to talk, Frenchman?"

Chapter 25

Allan Pinkerton read the wire again, wondering where he was going to find two detectives to send to Abilene in Kansas Territory. There was no way to avoid the request, for the president of the Kansas and Pacific Railroad was too important a customer to ignore when he personally wired for help after a series of train robberies.

"Sir?" John Wilson, his personal assistant, inquired from the office door.

"Yes, what is it?" Pinkerton replied angrily. He didn't appreciate being disturbed while he was thinking.

"There are two new agents here. They've just finished their schooling with Detective Andrews and are reporting for assignment."

Pinkerton's scowl was replaced by a more peaceful expression. *Just in the nick of time.*

Two young men, dressed identically in cheap brown business suits, boiled white shirts, fresh cardboard collars and bowler hats walked into the room.

"What are your names?" Pinkerton asked, skipping the formalities of a handshake to get right to the point.

The one on the left, six feet and two inches and heavy through the shoulders, took off his hat and said, "I'm Jack Ladd, sir."

"And you?" Pinkerton asked, glancing at the shorter man on the right.

"I'm John Whicher," he replied. He was roughly five feet, seven inches tall, thin and wiry. Both men wore small, well-trimmed mustaches without beards. Allan Pinkerton was the only man in the Pinkerton Detective Agency allowed to sport a full beard, by right of ownership.

"I understand you've completed your training as detectives for this agency."

"Yes, sir," the taller man replied.

"I have an immediate assignment for you. The Kansas and Pacific Railroad has been held up three times in the past few weeks east of Abilene, twice successfully. Over eight thousand in gold was taken. The president of the railroad informs me that the perpetrators wear white robes and silken hoods, embroidered with some sort of emblem representing a coiled snake."

Jack Ladd slowly shook his head. "That doesn't sound right, Mr. Pinkerton."

Pinkerton leaned back in his chair, pulled a cigar from his coat pocket and lit it, peering at Ladd through the smoke. "And why not, Mr. Ladd?"

Ladd's face turned a light shade of red. "What you are describing sounds like the costume of the Knights of the Golden Circle."

"Yes, I know. What leads you to conclude the Knights can't be involved in these rail holdups?"

"First of all, they're primarily based in the southeast, not so far north as Abilene, Kansas. And secondly, they've never been involved in train robberies to my knowledge. An occasional arson or the murder of a carpetbagger has officially been blamed on them, but nothing in the way of outright robbery, as far as I know. I find it out of character."

Pinkerton nodded, a look of approval on his face. "You are remarkably well informed for a new man. You are right, for the most part. The Knights have been most active around Natchez Under the Hill down in Mississippi, and up until now they haven't been guilty of outright theft at gunpoint. What we have to find out is if they are changing their ways, or if we dealing with a rogue element within the society that branched out on its own."

"Yes, sir," Ladd said.

"I want both of you to take the train to Abilene. I'll make arrangements for you to ride the Kansas and Pacific, to guard any shipments of money consigned by the army or Kansas banks."

Pinkerton stood up and walked around the desk. "Now, go to the armory and pick out your weapons, both handguns and long guns. I want you to have the very latest available for this assignment."

Ladd and Whicher boarded the Union Pacific Railroad toward Abilene, as the Kansas and Pacific did not operate a Chicago line, where the home offices of the Pinkerton Detective Agency were located.

Jack Ladd pulled a chrome-plated pistol from his shoulder holster to examine it before the locomotive crossed into Kansas. "I really like this Smith and Wesson American Model," he told Whicher, pushing a knob on the side of the pistol so it broke open like a shotgun. "See how quick it is to reload? A Colt would take twice as long."

Whicher nodded. "It's a right fine piece. And those new model 1873 Winchesters are pretty good. The new type of cartridges they fire are almost twice as powerful as the old ones."

Ladd grunted his agreement. "That's one

thing the Pinkertons do for their agents—give us good weapons to work with."

"Yeah, but I'm disappointed with our assignment," Whicher said.

"Why?" Ladd asked, holstering his pistol and turning in his seat to gaze at his partner.

"I was sort of hoping we'd get to go undercover in the Molly Maguire investigation."

"You mean those shaft explosions set off by mine laborers who want more money?"

"That's what they say is the cause, but I'm not so sure. To me, it sounds more like they're common criminals trying to extort money from the owners."

Ladd grinned. "That's the company line. Mr. Pinkerton never met a boss he didn't like, nor a common laborer he held above contempt."

Whicher frowned. "Are you saying that's wrong?"

Ladd wagged his head. "Of course not. But think about it. The Pinkerton Agency always sides with management, and as agents we're sent in to break up strikes and arrest troublemakers."

"So?"

"It strikes me as funny because almost all of the detectives in the agency come from labor backgrounds. Certainly none of us that I know of come from management families."

Whicher looked out the window. "Sometimes I think you think too damn much, Jack."

Their train chugged into Abilene, after two long days of travel. Ladd took a notepad from his pocket and glanced at it. "Our instructions are to introduce ourselves to the town marshal, Bill Hickok, and to the county sheriff, Roy Jones."

They climbed stiffly with their luggage into a ramshackle buggy taking passengers into town.

"You lookin' fer the marshal?" the wagon driver asked.

"Yes," Whicher said. "A Mr. Hickok, I believe."

The driver grinned, showing yellow stubs of teeth. "You ain't gonna find him in no office. You'd have better luck goin' to the Bull's Head Saloon."

Ladd pulled out a pocket watch, frowning. "But it's only ten o'clock in the morning."

"Yeah. One of the marshal's favorite sayin's is 'There's only two times a man should drink. When the sun's up an' when it's down.' "

Ladd and Whicher walked into the Bull's Head Saloon and stood just inside the batwings for a moment to let their eyes adjust to the darkness of the room.

"What's that smell?" whispered Whicher, his nose wrinkling.

Ladd made a face. "Smells like stale beer, whiskey and something real foul." He glanced at Whicher. "You don't suppose there's a dead body here somewhere that's been overlooked?"

A man behind the bar, sporting a waxed handlebar mustache, looked up when he saw them enter.

"Come on in, gentlemen. In spite of the looks of the place, we're open for business. It's early for all the cleanin' to be done yet."

Ladd and Whicher approached the bar, taking notice of a man wearing a buckskin jacket sitting at a corner table, nursing a beer mug brimming with red liquid.

"Howdy," the bartender said. "I'm Ben Thompson, an' this is Wild Bill Hickok," he said, inclining his head toward the only occupied table.

"Hello," Ladd said. "I'm Jack Ladd and this is John Whicher. We're detectives with the Pinkerton Agency, and we've come to introduce ourselves to Marshal Hickok."

As Hickok looked up, Ladd noted his eyes were already bloodshot and bleary. The lawman gave a lopsided grin. "Ah, gentlemen from the eye that never sleeps?" he inquired, parroting the agency's slogan.

Ladd walked over to the table and stuck out his hand. "Yes, sir. We've been assigned to guard the Kansas and Pacific Railroad for the next few weeks, until this business with hooded train robbers is wrapped up."

"You mean the Ghost Riders?" Thompson asked, chuckling as if there were something about the name he found amusing.

"Ghost Riders?" Whicher was puzzled.

Hickok grinned. "Yeah. That's the moniker hung on the bastards by some newspaper in Kansas City. Seems the first time they rustled some cattle, one of the cowboys who got away came running into town yelling his head off about some white ghosts who stole their beeves and shot down a couple of drovers. There was this newspaper gent in town who'd come to interview me that week, and he figured it'd be a nice title for his piece. Catchy. The name just kinda stuck."

"Do you think the thieves are members of the Knights of the Golden Circle, Marshal?" Ladd wondered as he took a chair across from Hickok.

Hickok waved the notion away. "I don't know nothing about 'em. Ain't in my jurisdiction. You'd have to ask Sheriff Roy Jones about that—if you can find him when he ain't off fishing someplace instead of tending to sheriffing business."

He drained his glass and motioned to Thompson for a refill.

Thompson looked at Ladd and Whicher. "You boys drinkin' anything this mornin'?"

"Do you have any coffee?" Whicher asked.

"Not likely," Thompson said. "This is a saloon. It ain't no boardin' house."

"You might try the red wine," Hickok said. "I heartily recommend it."

"We haven't had breakfast yet," Ladd said. "Do you know where we might be able to find Sheriff Jones?"

Thompson thought a moment. "If he's in town, you might run into him over at Maude's place. She serves a pretty fair breakfast and he's been known to take an early noonin' over there on occasion."

As Ladd and Whicher got up, Hickok spoke to them. "Good luck with your ghost hunting boys. You're gonna need it, but don't be expecting 'em to live up to their name. The only man who's managed to put a bullet through any ghosts around here is Doc Leo LeMat. Him and his partner, they killed two of 'em on the way to Abilene. Folks have decided maybe they ain't really ghosts after all."

"LeMat?" Ladd asked. He turned to Whicher. "We should interview him. Maybe he can tell us how they operate."

"He's over at the Drover's Inn, on Main Street," Hickok said. "You can't miss him. He'll be the citified dandy in the fancy dress coat hanging around with a short gent who looks like a sailor."

"Thanks for your help, Marshal," Ladd said, then followed Whicher through the batwings.

Chapter 26

Carl tied his horse in the alley behind the Drover's Inn. A clear night sky alive with winking stars gave him a clear view of the back stairway into the hotel. Wearing his soiled duster to hide his shotgun, his sweat-stained derby pulled low over his face, he felt certain no one had recognized him riding the dark back streets from Maude's to the Drover's, nor had anyone seen him turn into the alleyway. By his rough guess, it was half an hour away from midnight.

The night clerk, asleep at his desk with his head on his arms, didn't stir when Carl opened the register. He ran his stubby finger down the page until he came to Dr. Leo LeMat, room 12. No windows were lit on the top floor. LeMat was surely asleep by now. Carl meant to kill him in bed, a fate LeMat deserved for sneaking up behind him at the Bull's Head. If circumstances allowed, LeMat would taste the blade of his Arkansas toothpick moments after Carl broke down the door. Or a chest full of shotgun pellets if the sneaky son of a bitch came out with a gun before Carl could reach his bedside with the knife.

Despite his bulk, Pickins walked softly to the bottom of the steps and began a slow climb to the third floor, covering his progress with the scattergun. Weather-worn wooden stairs creaked under his weight, but with distant gunshots and music coming from the Devil's Addition, no one would notice unless someone saw him on the stairway.

You're a dead man, LeMat, he thought, eagerly awaiting the time when the cowardly sawbones woke up to a shaft of razor-sharp steel embedded in his heart.

Turning at the second-floor landing, he made the last part of his ascent soundlessly, ending at a thin door leading into the top-floor hallway. He twisted the knob and found it unlocked.

Glass-globed candles illuminated the hall. Counting numbers on inner doorways, Carl spotted number twelve at the far end. No light came from the cracks below any of the doors.

He's asleep, Carl told himself. *Perfect timing.* Passing the shotgun to his left hand, he pulled the knife from his boot.

As he crept down the hallway on the balls of

his feet, shadows from flickering candles made his silhouette dance on papered walls. Carl passed several doors, and heard a man snore deeply in one of the rooms.

He could see the tarnished brass number twelve atop one of the door frames only a few yards away. All was quiet, save for the snoring behind him, as he crept past room number eleven.

I'll throw my shoulder against the door, he thought, having no doubts that he could break it open easily. The room would be totally dark . . . he'd have to look for the bed and rush toward it as fast as he could. LeMat wouldn't be expecting him, probably figuring he was still in jail.

Carl came to room 12 and bunched his muscles, ready to send all his weight crashing through. The lock bolt would give way and then he'd be inside, ready to have his revenge at last, after brooding about it all during the previous night in jail. No one had ever drawn a gun on Carl Pickins and lived to brag about it. He rested his thumb on the shotgun's twin hammers, prepared to cock them the moment he was in the room.

Something made him hesitate . . . not a sound, for the hallway was silent. He sensed someone close by, a vague feeling with no explanation for it.

"*Batard,*" a feathery voice whispered behind him.

Carl jerked his head around to see who was there. A very short man in a pale sleeping gown smiled up at him in the most curious way. An old scar ran the length of one of his cheeks.

"Who the hell . . . ?" A metal object gleamed in the candles' faint light, sweeping toward his ribs with blinding speed.

A white-hot pain jolted through Carl's side. He tried to bring his shotgun around to blast the grin off this stranger's scarred face, but pain rendered him too weak to move. He took a staggering step forward.

Carl had opened his mouth to cry out, when suddenly a powerful hand clamped over his lips. And in the same instant he felt a new agony slice into his belly.

He fell to his knees, dropping his shotgun and knife to the floor, reeling back and forth while something warm and wet spilled over his belt.

"You like the knife?" the little man whispered. "*Bon.* So do I."

A ripping sound, accompanied by more pain searing upward to Carl's chest. Carl reached for the hand covering his mouth and the one holding the knife, clawing for them with curled fingers, his eyes bulging from their sockets.

"*Morte*, stupid one. Die slowly."

Carl slumped against the wall on his rump, finally able to speak, for the hand sealing his lips was gone. "Who . . . the hell . . . are you?" he croaked, feeling faint, gasping for breath.

"I am called Jacques. But what does a name matter now?"

"I got . . . no . . . quarrel . . . with you."

"Ah, but you do, *mon ami*. You have disturbed my slumber, and you came here to kill my friend, Dr. Leo LeMat."

The door to number 12 flew open. Carl saw a fuzzy image standing in the doorway, holding a gun.

"What is it, Jacques? Wait a minute . . . I recognize him now. He's Carl Pickins, the man who tried to shoot the bartender last night."

Carl's agony was too great to allow him anger when he saw LeMat. It was all he could do to breathe now.

"He will never try to shoot anyone again, *mon ami*. I have cut out one of his kidneys and part of his liver. He's bleeding to death. What a mess! He was coming after you with a knife and a shotgun. I felt I had no choice . . ."

Carl gazed down at his stomach. Blood was pouring from a gash across his right side and abdomen. And there was more, a thing he could not fully comprehend—coils of squirming purple snakes were crawling out of his belly, slithering into his lap.

"It would appear his intestines have decided to abandon him during his final hours," LeMat said, a voice Carl had difficulty hearing due to a strange ringing in his ears.

"*Oui.* It is not my fault. The *batard* turned around while my blade was in him, a very foolish thing to do. I will insist to Marshal Hickok that Mr. Pickins chose a bad time to move like a ballerina, twirling on his toes . . ."

Carl began slipping toward unconsciousness, wondering why the little man was making a joke of his knife wounds. If he had the strength to jerk his pistol free, he would kill LeMat and his grinning companion.

"We can't tell Hickok or Sheriff Jones about this, Jacques. You'll have to carry his body downstairs by the back way and get rid of him somehow. Suspicions about me and my reputation with a gun are already causing problems. I must finish my portrait of Hickok."

"You sons . . . of . . . bitches!" Carl groaned, making a feeble attempt to draw his revolver.

"But *mon ami*, he is making too much noise. Someone will surely hear me taking him downstairs—unless I can find a way to make him stop talking."

"Tie a cloth over his mouth," LeMat said.

"I have a better idea."

Carl saw the little man's face close to his, then a stinging sensation erupted on one side of his head. Seconds later a pulpy object was stuffed roughly into his mouth.

"You shouldn't have cut off his ear, Jacques. A cloth would have worked just as well."

"Where he is going, *mon ami*, he will have no use for either of his ears. A grave will be a very quiet place."

Carl attempted to spit out the ear, before a black fog enveloped him. He felt himself being carried away, lifted as if he weighed nothing.

Justin Davis was leaning against a porch post in front of the Broken Spoke in the Devil's Addition when he saw an unusual sight moving slowly down the street. A claybank dun gelding walked with its head lowered, trailing its reins. But what Justin saw lashed over the gelding's saddle stopped him cold, as he was about to raise a bottle of rotgut whiskey to his lips. He spoke to a cowboy seated on a bench behind him.

"Lookee yonder, Tooter! There's a dead man tied to that loose horse. Blood's all over his saddle too, only I can't get no fix on what's dragging the ground underneath him."

"Them's his guts, Justin. Somebody cut that poor son of a bitch's belly wide open. Looks like you'd know guts when you see 'em. Ain't you never killed no hog at butcherin' time?"

"Jesus Gawd-a'mighty, Tooter! Who'd go an' do a thing like that?"

"Some feller who was real pissed off at the guy on the dun. Sure as hell am glad he didn't have no grudge against me, whoever the hell he is."

"Better tell Marshal Hickok."

"You tell him. I'm busy drinkin' whiskey. You act like you ain't never seen no dead man in this town before. Go count them tombstones on Boot Hill if'n you got any doubts. This ain't no place fer a man who can't handle hisself."

"I'll go fetch the marshal. Seems like one of us oughtta do somethin'."

"Let the poor bastard have his last ride through Devilstown, Justin. Hickok's prob'ly busy drinkin' an' playin' poker anyhow, an' I sure as hell wouldn't want to be the one disturbs him."

The gelding plodded past the Broken Spoke. Justin looked on in amazement. Where else could a visiting cowboy see a sight like this without having it cause a ruckus?

"I still say somebody needs to tell the marshal, Tooter. There's a dead man ridin' a horse down Texas Street. Looks like he'd wanna know."

"Hickok don't give a damn 'bout nothin' but pretty whores an' winnin' at cards. I reckon he cares a whole lot 'bout red wine too." Tooter hesitated, scratching his beard stubble, "Course, if'n it were a stray dog . . ."

The claybank moved farther away. More men idling in front of saloons took notice of the bloody corpse.

"Hey, boys!" someone shouted. "That looks like ol' Carl Pickins tied to a horse there."

"Is he dead? Or just dead drunk?" another asked.

"Deader'n a horseshoe nail, what with his guts hangin' out."

"Ol' Carl finally got what was comin' to him. Let's have another drink an' celebrate him passin' on. Kansas is rid of one more sorry son of a bitch now, if that's him."

"It's him all right. Pass me that jug."

Chapter 27

As the hour approached noon, Leo and Jacques made their way to the veranda of the Drover's Hotel. Leo had invited Hickok to meet them there for lunch prior to his sitting at one o'clock.

"There's Monsieur Hickok," Jacques said, pointing toward a table at the back of the veranda. Leo saw the marshal sitting with his back to the wall again, so no one could walk behind Hickok in passing.

"He's a very careful man, *mon ami*," Leo said.

"Or one who has made very many enemies," Jacques replied.

"Howdy, gents," Hickok said in a jovial voice when they came to his table, evidently well into his daily consumption of wine.

Jacques and Leo shook the marshal's hand and took seats across from Hickok.

"Good morning, Marshal," Leo said, while

Jacques merely nodded a greeting. "It's a beautiful spring day in Kansas."

Hickok scowled briefly. "There's nothing beautiful about Kansas." His frown relaxed when he saw a young woman strolling past the Drover's. "Except for the women. They grow 'em right here. Must be all the beef. Puts meat on their bones."

Jacques chuckled. "Indeed, Marshal Hickok. They do an excellent job of breeding fine women here."

A waitress approached their table and placed handwritten menus in front of them. Leo noticed she was careful to stay out of Hickok's reach, watching him warily from the corner of her eye.

"What will you gentlemen be having for lunch?" she asked tentatively.

Leo looked at Jacques, to whom he typically left the ordering of meals.

"We'll have a pot of the special coffee to start with. Just ask the chef. He'll know which one I mean. Then, filet of brook trout almondine with plenty of sliced tomatoes and skillet-fried potatoes. And for dessert, apple pie, heated of course, and more coffee." Jacques looked across at the marshal. "And how about you, Marshal Hickok?"

"That sounds pretty good to me, though I don't usually eat much until supper." He patted his abdomen, "My gut's been kinda acting up lately."

Leo almost advised him to avoid the intake of so much wine, especially when his stomach was empty, and to eat more than one meal a day, until he thought better of it. About the only thing worse than having a casual acquaintance ask for medical advice was for a self-important physician to offer it unsolicited.

Jacques spoke to the waitress, "That will be three orders of the trout, please."

She bowed politely, and began to walk toward the kitchen. Hickok's hand shot out, grabbing a fistful of her dress where it covered her hips.

"Little lady, how 'bout bringing me another glass of this here wine? I'm still thirsty." As he spoke, he moved his hand in a circle over her buttocks.

Her face flamed red and she squirmed out of his reach, stalking into the hotel.

Leo noticed Jacques's irritation over the marshal's rude treatment of the girl; however, Jacques said nothing, for which Leo was thankful. More important to them both than a slight shown to a young waitress was finishing Hickok's portrait.

"Marshal, did you have an uneventful evening?" Leo asked, to quickly move their discussion away from what Jacques thought of the marshal's manners.

"Wasn't too bad," Hickok replied, glancing up with keen disappointment on his face when an older waitress, her gray hair twisted into a tight bun, brought his wine and placed it in front of him.

After she gave Leo and Jacques cups, the woman filled them with coffee from a large carafe and left it on the table. Leo was certain he recognized a familiar aroma, despite all that trouble between Jacques and the hotel cook.

Leo took a sip from his cup. "Jacques, this is chicory coffee, and it's very good."

Jacques offered a secretive smile. "Just wait until you taste the entrée, monsieur."

"What've you been up to, my friend?"

Jacques wore a satisfied expression now. "I concluded that if we were to stay here for any length of time, it would be unbearable to have to eat the terrible food that would-be chef was preparing. So, I decided to take matters into my own hands and make friends with him. Last evening, I approached him and we . . . shared recipes. Today, the brook trout we are having are actually Jacques's *trout à la Ponchartrain,* as I learned to cook it in New Orleans. The chef was so appreciative to learn the correct use of certain spices and herbs he's allowed me to make our coffee every morning and will serve it to us on request."

Hickok pulled a long, black cigar from his coat pocket and ran it under his nose, inhaling loudly. After a moment, he stuck it in his mouth and lit it with a lucifer he struck on the butt of one of his Colts.

Leo thought Hickok looked bored, and realized the marshal wasn't interested in any conversation that wasn't about him. He was about to ask Hickok to relate some of his early exploits, when the lawman's eyes fixed on something. He sat up a bit straighter in his chair.

"Looks like we're about to have some company, gentlemen," Hickok said, inclining his head toward two men in brown suits walking toward their table.

Noticing the stern expressions on the strangers' faces, Leo opened his coat and got ready to reach for his LeMat. "Trouble?" he asked in a low voice.

"No, they're just a couple of Pinkerton men who've been all over town asking a lot of damn fool questions about those Ghost Riders."

Leo relaxed and leaned back in his chair.

Jack Ladd and John Whicher stood rather stiffly in front of their table and introduced themselves.

"Boys," Hickok said, "this here is Dr. Leo

LeMat and his friend Jacques LeDieux, the two men I told you about this morning who put those train robbers forked-end-up the other day."

"Have a seat, gentlemen," Leo said. "Would you like some coffee?"

"I could sure use some," Ladd said, shoving the empty cup in front of him toward Leo.

"Sounds good to me," Whicher said.

Leo filled two cups from the carafe. "This is chicory and it has a distinctive taste. If you don't like it, we can get you Arbuckle's from our waitress."

Ladd took a tentative sip, made a slightly sour face, and added several heaping teaspoons of sugar. "Dr. LeMat, we had a long talk with Sheriff Roy Jones this morning over breakfast. He told us that he'd received a wire concerning you from Heck Thomas over at Fort Smith."

"Yes?" Leo asked, remembering the scene Jones had caused the other night when he was with Pauline.

Whicher spoke up. "It seems Thomas doesn't think much of your reputation. He thinks you're not much more than a hired killer."

Leo spread his palms. "Marshal Thomas's opinion is not of the least concern to me, Mr. Ladd. Though it's true that I've killed a few men over the years, I have never so much as been charged with any crime, let alone convicted of one, so I'd suggest you get to the point."

"We simply found it rather odd that a man with your reputation happened to be riding on a train when the bandits struck," Whicher remarked.

"A coincidence, perhaps," Leo said. "As I'm sure you recall, my associate and I killed two of the highwaymen, saving whatever contents were in the safe from falling into their hands."

Hickok watched the exchange with mounting interest. Evidently he hadn't heard about Leo's reputation with a gun, until now.

"Anyway, we'll let that coincidence sit for a while," Ladd said. "What can you tell us about the method these Ghost Riders use to rob the trains?"

Leo took a drink of his coffee, watching Ladd over the rim of his cup. "Apparently, they jump the trains at a water stop, when the engines have already begun to slow. Several of the robbers attack the engine to subdue the engineer, while others simultaneously rob passenger cars and the baggage car where the most valuable shipments are kept. It seems these men are well advised on how to proceed, though they are not well disciplined. Facing stiff resistance in the form of flying lead from my friend Jacques and myself, the remaining bandits fled without putting up any fight whatsoever."

"*Oui*," Jacques added. "The cowardly thieves ran away like scalded dogs rather than face us." He glanced at Hickok with a scornful look on his face. "I have a rather low opinion of Kansas robbers, Marshal, for they have no backbone."

"What've you got in mind to halt the robberies, Mr. Ladd?" Leo asked.

Ladd reached over and refilled his cup, evidently used to the bitter taste of chicory now. "We'll ride every train carrying payrolls or large sums of money. If the robbers hit, then we'll be ready for them."

"What about the rustling they've been doing?" Hickok asked.

Ladd spoke quietly. "That isn't any of our business. We've been hired by the railroad to protect their shipments and employees. If the cattlemen want protection, they'll have to take that up with Mr. Pinkerton."

As their graying waitress arrived with their food, the two Pinkerton men stood up. "Thanks for your help, Dr. LeMat. We'll let you get on with your lunch now," Ladd said. He tipped his hat and added, "Good day, gentlemen," then he led Whicher off the veranda, heading toward the Cattleman's Bank.

Hickok wagged his head as he pulled his

plate of trout toward him. "Damned Pinkertons," he said. "They're meaner than a snoozing grizzly bear, but most of 'em don't have a lick of sense."

"What do you mean?" asked Leo.

Hickok pointed his fork after the retreating detectives. "Going around telling everybody what they plan to do ain't exactly the smartest thing. Hell, everyone figures the Ghost Riders are from around here, so they're bound to find out about the trap set for 'em on them money trains."

Leo nodded. "Perhaps the detectives are not so dumb. It could be that they want the bandits to find out, hoping it will keep them from attempting further robberies."

"Maybe, but I think they're wrong. Them Ghost Riders aren't cowards, in spite of the way they acted when you surprised 'em the other day. Once they hear the trains are gonna be guarded, they'll come prepared. With enough money at stake, whoever's behind 'em will only hire more gunmen—some boys who *know* how to shoot."

Hickok stopped talking long enough to stuff a forkful of trout into his mouth. After a moment he blinked, and then he smiled, looking across the table at Jacques. "Damn! This is good.

Never tasted a fish quite like this. Most of it tastes too damn fishy."

Jacques grinned. *"Oui, monsieur.* Thank you. It seems even a cranky cowboy cook can be trained to prepare a delicacy."

Chapter 28

After stopping by Drover's Supply in Abilene to add a pair of shotguns to their arsenal, Jack Ladd and John Whicher packed their weapons in a large canvas duffel bag. They had picked up two American Arms ten-gauge express guns, along with four boxes of 00-buckshot shells.

"Do you think this'll be enough?" Whicher asked.

Ladd flashed a humorless grin. "If four boxes of shells don't get the job done, it won't get done by us, partner," he said, stuffing the rifles and shotguns in the canvas tote. Their pistols were carried in shoulder holsters under their suit coats.

They boarded the eastbound Kansas and Pacific, intending to ride it toward the rising sun to Kansas City, where transaction money for cattle buyers would be transferred from a Wells, Fargo and Company office to the train. They then

planned to accompany the specified train back
on its westward journey the following day, riding in the baggage car equipped with a large
Tru-Lock safe to guard the shipment of cash
until it could be deposited in the Cattleman's
Bank in Abilene.

They booked tickets on a Pullman car to get
as much sleep as was possible on the rolling,
jolting train. Hastily laid tracks to new cattle
markets in Kansas Territory were often loosened
by badly overloaded cattle cars, causing a sway-
ing motion passengers found annoying, even
dangerous when loose rail spikes allowed a
train to jump the tracks. Over a hundred miles
of uneven rails lay between Abilene and Kansas
City, a grim fact Jack Ladd had worried about
since they'd been given this assignment. A gang
of clever thieves had dozens of remote places
where they could pull up a section of rail spikes,
and there were always water stops to consider
as perfect spots to stage a robbery.

As the train labored into Kansas City following a painfully slow seven-hour trip, the line of
cars was slowed by a screech of brakes and a
giant hiss of steam. Ladd bounded off the car
as the locomotive came to a complete halt, striding into the station master's office, followed by
a yawning John Whicher.

He showed his Pinkerton credentials and said, "I'd like you to get a wagonload of sandbags, about a hundred ought to do it. Then I want them piled around the inside walls of the baggage car coupled to tomorrow afternoon's Abilene run."

The stationmaster cocked his head. "And just who's gonna pay for all this?" he asked.

Ladd leaned over the man's desk. "I'm acting on direct orders from Allan Pinkerton, who spoke personally with Jessie Van Buren, President of the Kansas and Pacific. If you'd like to wire Mr. Van Buren and tell him you're reluctant to help . . ."

"Oh no, sir. I'm sure that won't be necessary," the man replied. "Is there anything else you'll be needing?"

"Now that you mention it: Find a carpenter, and have him cut small rifle holes in both walls of the car above the level of those sandbags. Then I want the barred windows boarded up until the car is sealed up tighter than a gnat's ass. And while you're at it, send a boy over to the nearest general store for this," he added, handing the man a written list of supplies.

"Yes, sir," the stationmaster said, hurrying from the depot as if he wanted to get away before Jack made anymore demands.

"Jesus, Jack," Whicher said. "We're gonna

suffocate in that car. It's gonna get as hot as Hades without any way for the air to circulate."

"We'll leave the baggage car door open a bit while the train is moving. There's no need to keep it shut unless the train slows or it's stopped by bandits. Then we can slam it real quick and bolt it from the inside. Once we fight the robbers off, I've brought a portable telegraph machine. All we have to do is tie a line into the wire running alongside the tracks and we can telegraph the army which way the bastards make their escape. With any luck, they'll be able to intercept them before they can go to ground."

Whicher removed his bowler hat and scratched his head. "Looks like you've thought of just about everything, Jack."

"It's a good plan, if they stick to what they've done in the past. At any rate, it'll be damned hard for them to get to us in a sandbagged baggage car, and we'll have a clear shot at them no matter which side they come from."

The conductor cried, "All aboard!" All modifications to the baggage car Jack asked for had been made. He brought two picnic baskets from the station and hoisted them inside the car.

"What's that?" Whicher asked.

"I've laid us up plenty of food and water, just in case they try to starve us out. Hell, with this amount of grub, we're set for several days. Besides, I was hungry. The food in this end of Kansas City is lousy."

A steam whistle blew as the Kansas and Pacific westbound started on its way to Abilene.

Sloan Wilson was getting tired of waiting. Even though it was early spring, the temperature was still in the low nineties, hinting of the hell Kansas was going to be later in the summer. He was suffocating inside the stupid hood and cloak he was told to wear.

"Damn it, Clyde. Where the hell is that train? I thought you said it'd be here by now," he grumbled.

"You know trains, Sloan. They don't hardly ever run on time. It'll be here."

They were waiting near Junction City, the last water stop on the rail line to Abilene. The location had been Sloan's idea. They'd heard there were going to be a couple of Pinkerton men guarding the train, and he figured they would let down their guard after the final water stop, thinking they were safe from being robbed. This bit of news about Pinkertons came from Maude Day, along with another grim tidbit: Someone had killed Carl Pickins with a knife, something Sloan wouldn't have believed was possible if he hadn't heard it himself from Maude.

Just past a bend in the tracks, he'd tied two sticks of dynamite together and placed them under a rail with a two-minute fuse. Leaving Tully with the dynamite, Sloan, Clyde and Jess waited farther down the tracks, where the baggage car should end up after the train ran off the tracks.

Finally in the distance, a whistle sounded, and Sloan saw faint outlines of the engine in the moonlight.

As the train neared, Sloan took off his hat and waved it at Tully, signaling him to light the fuse and hightail it to join them.

Jack Ladd was standing in the open doorway of the baggage car, leaning against the wall smoking a cigar, enjoying the slight relief the moving air gave him from the stifling heat inside.

Jack was feeling pretty good—downright confident, in fact. They'd made their last water stop and it looked like this cash shipment would make it through without any attempt on the part of the so-called Ghost Riders to intercept it. Jack was also planning to explain his ideas on how to fortify baggage cars in the future to Mr. Pinkerton. Perhaps he'd get a promotion to senior detective out of this, if things worked right.

The glint of moonlight on metal off to his right caught his attention.

"Quick, John, hand me those field glasses!"

"What's the matter?"

"Just give 'em here!"

After a moment staring through the binoculars, focusing in on a spot in spite of the sway of the train, Jack whispered, "Oh, shit."

"What is it, Ladd? What the hell do you see?"

"Looks like three men wearing white robes sitting on horses over in that copse of trees, though it's too dark to be absolutely certain."

"White robes?"

Jack gritted his teeth. Sometimes John could be so dense that he wondered how Whicher had made it through Pinkerton detective training. "White robes, John. I see them clearly now, and they are staying well away from the tracks. I've got a gut feeling we're about to experience a real sudden stop. Now help me get this door shut and grab your guns."

After they had the door shut and bolted, Jack backed into a corner piled with sandbags and braced himself with his arms.

"What are you doing?" Whicher asked.

"Get down, John! There isn't time to—"

Before he could finish his warning, Jack heard a thundering explosion from the front of the train.

Seconds later, the baggage car lurched to one side amid the tortured scream of twisting metal, rocking back and forth twice before turning half-way around and finally coming to a grinding halt. Both men were thrown to their knees on the wooden floor of the car.

"Goddamn it!" John yelped. "I tore open my knee. I'm bleeding real bad, Jack. Help me."

Jack scrambled on hands and knees to the gun rack next to the safe and grabbed his rifle and shotgun and a box of shells. "You better hope that's all you get, Johnny boy, 'cause we're about to find out if these sandbags'll stop bullets."

A volley of gunshots rang out and several slugs drilled holes in the wooden sides of the car, whining by the detectives' ears. Others thudded loudly as they plowed into the piled sandbags.

Jack peeked through one of the rifle slots and saw the four men riding up to the baggage car. He raised his express gun and stuck the barrel out the hole.

The gun exploded against his shoulder, knocking him half a step backward, reminding him not to pull both triggers at the same time.

A shrill scream from outside was followed by a harsh grunt as one of the robbers toppled off his horse, landing on his back beside the rails.

261

Jack reloaded quickly and fired his express gun again, but the range was too great and he missed another moving target. When smoke from the shotgun billowed back into the baggage car, filling it with the acrid smell of cordite, Jack discovered a shortcoming to his plans. With no way to escape, gunsmoke was going to make it difficult to breathe if the fight lasted very long.

The three remaining gunmen opened up on the car, peppering it with what seemed like hundreds of slugs as John and Jack fired back through rifle slots.

Minutes later, with the air in the car becoming increasingly foul from the gunsmoke, all gunfire from outside abruptly ceased.

Jack slowly raised his head and peered out the gunport, but he could see no sign of the holdup men.

"Do you think they've given up?" asked John hopefully.

"Not on your life, partner. Get ready. I don't know what they're up to, but I don't like this silence."

As John started to reply, Jack held up his hand. He thought he heard something just outside the door. He cocked his head, listening intently.

Suddenly, he knew what it was.

"Get down!" he yelled. "Dynamite!"

He grabbed John and dragged him quickly to a far corner of the car. He hunkered down and began to pull sandbags around them until they were all but buried beneath them.

Half a minute later a tremendous roaring sound filled Jack's ears, and a black hole opened up to swallow them both.

Chapter 29

Sloan jerked off his sweaty hood and threw it away, thankful to finally be rid of it. He shed his silk robe and tossed it down while they led a spare horse that once belonged to Jess Miller, now loaded with money bags, away from the scene of the train wreck.

Clyde rode beside Sloan while Tully stayed a quarter mile back to make certain they weren't being followed.

"How much you reckon we got, Sloan?" Clyde asked, removing his own hood and cloak and stuffing them into his saddlebags.

"Thousands in paper money, maybe as much as ten thousand. Could be more, an' then there's the sacks of gold an' silver. I got no idea how much the take's gonna be, but it's damn sure a plenty."

"Too bad about Jess."

"He rode into a swarm of buckshot, Clyde.

He didn't have a helluva lot of sense. Tully ain't much smarter'n he was, if you ask me."

"We're rich as kings now, soon as Mr. Bell gives us our share."

Sloan had been thinking about just that ever since they blew open the safe to find it loaded with money. "We can be a helluva lot richer, Clyde, if you'll listen to me."

"What are you sayin', Sloan?"

"I'm sayin' we split this loot in half between the two of us tonight. Then we clear out for California."

"But what about Tully? An' Mr. Bell?"

"To hell with both of 'em. I'll ride back an' kill Tully. Then we head straight for San Francisco with all of this money. Old man Bell can't tell nobody what we done, 'cause he was behind all the robberies in the first place. If he sends that big nigra after us, we'll kill him too. Bell won't know we've pulled out till we've put a hundred miles behind us. We can be plumb out of Kansas in three days, ridin' through Colorado Territory with all them Rocky Mountains to hide us. We'll board a train in Denver with all this loot. A week, an' we're safe in California usin' different names, where won't nobody know us or recognize us. We get a fresh start as rich men."

Clyde was frowning. "Seems kinda cold-blooded, to shoot Tully. He was in on the job."

"You gettin' softhearted, Clyde? Think about spendin' all this damn money. Half of it'll be yours if Tully's out of the way, an' that's one less man who can tell the law what we done. We'll be free as birds in San Francisco, our pockets so full of cash we'll never be able to spend it all, even if we live to be a hundred."

"Sounds mighty nice. I always did· dream 'bout bein' rich."

"We are rich right now. All I'm sayin' is we make ourselves richer by cuttin' out Tully an' old man Bell. Nobody besides you an' me will ever know."

Clyde glanced over his shoulder, where Tully rode over the crest of a grassy moonlit hill. "I reckon it's all right with me, Sloan, only I ain't gonna shoot Tully myself. We was always friends."

"A man can't afford no friends when the stakes get too high. You keep ridin'. I'll swing back an' take care of Tully. We'll use his horse, an' Jess's, for spares so we can cover some ground tonight. We'll head up the Solomon River. That's empty country all the way to the Colorado line."

"Go ahead, Sloan. I'll keep leadin' this horse like there ain't nothin' wrong while you ride back to shoot Tully. I ain't sayin' I don't feel bad about this . . ."

"You'll get over it," Sloan said, handing over the reins to the spare horse. "Bein' rich will take your mind off a lot of things as soon as we get to California."

He rode up to Tully at a slow trot, reining his roan down to a walk. "Anybody behind us?" he asked.

Tully turned back in the saddle for a view of their backtrail, the very thing Sloan expected him to do.

"No sir, there ain't. Empty as a whiskey jug on Sunday mornin' behind us."

Sloan drew his Mason Colt .44–.40. "Also about as empty as your skull," he said quietly, aiming for Tully's chest.

Tully glanced over his shoulder. "What the hell do you mean by that?"

His answer was a single gunshot, echoing over dark hills around them. The force of a .44 slug charged by forty grains of gunpowder swept him out of the saddle when it struck his breastbone. His horse bolted away from the noise of the gun, tossing Tully's body over its rump before it lunged to the right at full speed.

Tully landed flat on his back, a strangled cry caught in his throat as blood pumped from a mortal wound below his ribs. He thrashed back and forth a moment in agony, then his limbs relaxed and he lay still.

Sloan swung down to make sure Tully was dead, yet he found the man was still breathing. He placed the cold muzzle of his pistol against Tully's forehead and pulled the trigger without hesitation.

"No witnesses," Sloan said, collecting his reins to mount the roan again. "Wasn't nothin' personal, Tully, but a man has to learn how to count . . . an' how to divide up money."

Chapter 30

Leo took Pauline by the arm to help her into the surrey. She'd packed a picnic lunch, promising to show him what she called the prettiest spot in Dickinson County. It was a place on the banks of the Solomon River where she said wildflowers grew in abundance. Leo had his sketch pad with him, hoping to sit Pauline among colorful spring flowers to craft preliminary drawings for a portrait he planned to do of her, if she would allow it.

As they pulled down Main Street, a medicine wagon with "Dr. Montescue's Magic Elixir" painted on the side came rolling into town from the east.

"Do you believe there can be any value to the elixirs traveling medicine men sell?" Pauline asked. "Some claim they are magic potions."

"The only thing magic about them is the way they make people part with hard-earned money for a bottle of sweetened water with strychnine or alcohol in it."

"They don't cure anything?"

"A professor of mine at the University of Pennsylvania once said, only half in jest, that God cures and the physician takes all the credit. That's the way it is with patent medicines. A patient takes some, gets better as he would have during the natural course of things, and believes it's the medicine cured him."

As the wagon drew abreast of the surrey, Leo glanced in the back. Two men were lying in the wagonbed. He couldn't quite see their faces, however he thought he recognized them by their dress, the identical brown suits worn by the Pinkertons he met at the Drover's.

"Hold on, there!" Leo called to the driver of the medicine wagon as he reined the surrey around.

He drove up beside the peddler's wagon. "What happened to those men in the back?" he asked.

The driver, a man dressed in the long black coat and top hat favored by many physicians in larger towns, replied, "The Kansas and Pacific train was held up last night. Robbers blew up the track and wrecked the train. These gents got blowed up in one of the cars. The conductor stopped me as I was driving along the tracks and he asked me to bring 'em here. They're hurt pretty bad."

Leo turned to Pauline. "Where's the closest doctor's office?"

She spoke to the driver. "Follow us. We'll show you the way." She pointed south. "Turn left at the next street—it's right around the corner."

Leo snapped the reins over the buggy horse's back, following Pauline's directions to a house with a shingle hanging on a post in the yard reading DR. SANDERS. He climbed down and hurried to the back of the medicine wagon to help the injured Pinkerton detectives while Pauline ran toward the house.

Jack Ladd appeared to be conscious, able to walk with his arm over the medicine peddler's shoulder, but John Whicher was completely out cold.

Pauline turned from the door, a look of dismay on her face. "Leo, Dr. Sanders's wife says he is away delivering Mrs. Calloway's baby. They live more than ten miles out of town."

"Ask her to let us in. These men need immediate attention," he said, cradling Whicher in his arms.

The doctor's wife showed them inside, where Leo put Whicher on an operating table. Ladd, with some assistance, was seated in a corner chair.

"Are you a surgeon, Dr. Montescue?" Leo asked, slipping off Whicher's coat and shirt.

"No, sir. I was trained by a steam healer, but it won't help with none of this." His face paled and Leo noticed sweat beading on his forehead. "Matter of fact," he said, wiping his face with a handkerchief, "I don't do so good when I see blood. I'm afraid I'm gonna have to leave."

Leo took his coat off and started rolling up his sleeves as he turned to Pauline. "You'll have to help me," he told her, as Montescue left the room.

She did not hesitate, taking off her straw hat and pushing the sleeves of her spring dress up her arms. "I'll try. What do you want me to do?"

"Let's see what we have to work with," he said, moving over to a cabinet with Dr. Sanders's wife looking on.

He found a bottle of carbolic acid and poured some in a washbasin. "Add a pitcher of hot water to this," he said to Pauline.

The doctor's wife brought a pitcher of water, and Leo began to wash his hands, dipping them in weak acid solution.

"Why are you doing this?" Pauline asked.

"What does washing your hands have to do with helping these men?"

"A doctor in Vienna named Semmelweiss has discovered that a way to prevent infection is to wash your hands, and a patient's wounds, in a diluted solution of carbolic acid. I learned of his writings while I was studying new methods of preventing childbed fever after my wife's death." He returned to the table and began to examine Whicher carefully.

Leo noted a large gash in Whicher's scalp, which was still oozing blood, though the major bleeding had stopped. He stripped off Whicher's pants and started to run his hands gently over the detective's body. He found the man had a broken left arm, between the elbow and wrist, along with numerous cuts and contusions. A foot-long splinter of wood stuck out of Whicher's left side like a well-aimed spear. Removing it safely would require great care and a piece of luck.

"Hand me that needle and suture, on the shelf next to the surgical instruments," Leo instructed.

Pauline handed him a needle and thread. Leo began to close the wound on Whicher's scalp. "While I finish here, would you check with Mr. Ladd to find out how badly he's hurt?"

She departed to question the other detective.

With the scalp wound closed, Leo turned his attention to the splinter in Whicher's abdomen. He poured carbolic acid solution all around the wound, cleaning off the dried blood as best he could, then he gently pulled out the piece of wood.

Pauline appeared at his side. "Mr. Ladd's injuries don't seem too serious. He says they're mainly cuts and bruises."

"Thanks. Now, if Mr. Whicher's luck holds, this splinter won't have pierced his bowels. It appears to have penetrated only muscle. Time will tell."

"What if it *has* gone into the bowels?" she asked.

"Then he's done for. I have never seen anyone survive that type of injury. Hold a cloth around the hole while I remove the rest of the splinters. It may bleed heavily, so I need to have you apply pressure while I probe the opening."

Pauline pressed a thick cloth over the bleeding wound, while Leo took a pair of forceps from Dr. Sanders's cabinet and gently probed the wound to see if it penetrated completely through the muscle layer of the abdomen.

"Mr. Whicher is in luck. After a few days of rather intense pain, and a month or more with his arm in a splint, he should be fit to resume the detective profession."

Leo stitched the abdominal wound closed before preparing a splint to Whicher's left arm. Both detectives had been fortunate to survive a train derailment. He would ask Ladd how it came about after he finished with Whicher's splint.

"What exactly happened, Mr. Ladd?" he asked as he cleaned a number of abrasions on Ladd's face and chest.

"The thieves put dynamite on the tracks just past Junction City. After the train derailed, they attacked us in the baggage car. They used dynamite. We were lucky as hell to get out of it alive."

"This particular bunch does seem to have a fondness for violence," Leo agreed.

"They must have used a considerable amount of explosive. I'd fortified the car with sandbags. We barely had time to cover ourselves before the explosion. What I can't figure out is why they didn't kill us when we were lying there unconscious. The conductor found me and woke me up to tell me they made off with all the money. The safe was blown open by the blast."

"It's possible the Pinkerton Agency's reputation saved your lives. Almost everyone in the outlaw profession should know by now that killing a Pinkerton detective leads to swift retaliation from Allan Pinkerton. I've read about it in several newspapers."

Ladd nodded. "I suppose that's true, according to what I've been told. How is John doing? Is he gonna be okay?"

"He'll take some time to heal, but eventually he'll be as good as new."

When Leo put the final bandage on Ladd's leg, the detective stuck out his hand. "Dr. LeMat, thank you for helping John and me. We've heard some tales about you and your gun, that you're a hired killer. A U.S. Marshal up in Fort Smith didn't have much good to say about you. Maybe you are a professional killer, but you took the time to patch up me and my partner. We owe you."

"It's the least I could do. Dr. Sanders is away delivering a baby. As to the tales you've heard, I wouldn't put much stock in them until you've heard both sides of the story."

"I'll tell you what, Doctor. I'm gonna wire Heck Thomas to tell him what you did today, after I get off a wire to the army about what happened. Thomas has got the wrong ideas about you."

"And I intend to tell my father what a good doctor you are," Pauline added, her eyes shining. "I hope to change his opinion of you as well."

Leo turned to Pauline. "I believe we have unfinished business on the banks of the Solomon River. There's a lunch in the floorboard of our surrey and it's going to waste. Let's wash the blood off our hands and put our efforts toward far more pleasant activities. These detectives can manage on their own now, until Dr. Sanders returns."

Chapter 31

Pauline directed Leo to a beautiful spot on the banks of the Solomon River, where lush green grasses spread to the edge of the water. Tall cottonwood trees grew in clusters beside the river, offering shade from the sun.

As Pauline unpacked her picnic basket, Leo examined the surrounding countryside with an artist's critical eye. This spot would be perfect for what he had in mind. There was a winding dirt road to give the painting depth, and beyond it he saw a field filled with a full rainbow of colors from blooming wildflowers; brilliant reds, yellows and golds, bold blues and vibrant purples. He was picking out a spot where he would seat Pauline in the midst of the flowers when she giggled and grabbed his arm.

"Come on, Doctor. Your picnic feast awaits," she said, leading him over to a quilted blanket she'd arranged under the tree.

"It looks delicious," he said.

She'd laid out fried chicken, potato salad, sweet pickles and two bottles of wine. Sitting next to the basket was a peach cobbler for dessert.

"I worked and slaved in the kitchen for hours to prepare this, and I did it just for you, Leo."

"It is wonderful, *'tite belle*," he said, briefly tracing her cheek with his fingertips. He sat on the quilt, opened the wine and poured them both glasses. Handing one to her, he touched them together in a toast. "To the most beautiful cook in Kansas," he said.

She laughed after taking a drink of wine. "You'd better try the chicken before you say that."

He began to eat, watching her as he chewed. Her chicken was passable, but he didn't dare tell her it would never compare to Jacques's more heavily spiced version.

"How do you like it?" Pauline asked.

"It may be the best chicken I've ever eaten."

She smiled. "Just wait until you get to the cobbler. I must admit my mother helped me with it, and she is known all over the county for her cobblers."

As they finished off the chicken and potato salad, they talked about what Pauline wanted from life. Leo was surprised to learn she wasn't at all interested in getting married or starting a family like most girls her age. She wanted to go to college. "I've dreamed of becoming a doctor. Assisting you with those wounded Pinkerton detectives helped make up my mind."

Leo hesitated. It was never easy to cast doubts on someone's dreams or aspirations, yet he felt compelled to warn her of the difficulties she faced.

"You have chosen a very difficult road for yourself. There were only a handful of women in my classes at the University of Pennsylvania, and they were treated harshly, forced to endure constant scorn . . . even outright ridicule."

"But you're not saying it cannot be done?" she asked.

"Oh, no. In fact, a graduate in my class joined the Union Army during the Civil War and became a battlefield heroine. She was later decorated by President Lincoln."

"What did she do?"

"During a famous battle, I believe it was Gettysburg, she dressed as a man and wandered on the battlefield while the fight was still engaged, dressing wounds, taking care of the injured on both sides." He chuckled. "It's said that though she was physically very homely, she received several proposals of marriage that day from men she ministered to under fire."

"That's what I want to do, to help people."

"It is a noble profession, Pauline, and I believe you will make a wonderful doctor." He waggled a finger at her. "But remember, do not give up when you are treated shabbily. Keep your chin up and do your best, and you will certainly prevail."

She sidled over to him on the quilt and put her arms around his neck in a warm hug. "Thank you, Leo. My father keeps telling me I'm crazy to want this."

Thinking he'd better do something before things got out of hand, Leo stood up and walked toward the field of wildflowers. "Come on, *cherie*, I want to place you among the beautiful flowers and make some sketches for a painting I'll do later."

She jumped to her feet and ran toward him. "You want to paint me?"

"Absolutely—here, among the flowers. A painting I will call 'Nature's Beauty' and will hang on my wall forever."

"Where do you want me?" she asked, excitedly twirling and dancing around him.

"Here," he said, pointing to a place where she could sit surrounded by color, where the road would be in the background, winding away from her toward the horizon. It would be perfect.

Leo gave her a glass of wine and sat fifteen yards from her, his sketch pad on his knee, with the sun over his left shoulder in order to catch the emerald color of her eyes, the slight ruby tinge to her cheeks and the highlights in her hair awakened by the sun.

He sketched for almost an hour, making notations on the pad regarding colors of the flowers so he could fill them in later. He refilled her wineglass several times, as well as his own, and soon they were both laughing and smiling from the effects of the wine, and the pleasure they felt in each other's company.

As he was putting the finishing touches on his drawing, two men appeared on the road, cresting a grassy hill where the trail made a bend. They were riding westward at a ground-eating trot, leading a pair of saddled horses with bulky canvas sacks tied over empty saddle seats. The men seemed to be in a hurry, their mounts coated with lather. And Leo noticed that they carried guns.

"Trouble," Leo said, tossing his sketching pad and charcoal aside. "Get up, Pauline! Run for those trees."

"But why, Leo?" she asked, looking at the horsemen. "They're only cowboys."

He leapt to his feet, seizing her wrist, jerking

her roughly off the grass. "No time to argue. Run!"

He pulled her toward the cottonwoods, keeping an eye on the pair of riders. Leo felt Pauline draw back, stumbling now and then until they reached the cover of thick tree trunks beside the river.

"What's wrong with you, Leo?" There were tears on her face and she shrunk away from him when he let go of her arm, noting the look of terror in her eyes.

Thinking about the outlaws, Leo felt himself on the verge of losing control to violent urges. He felt the pressure building inside him, threatening to explode. "Lie down and keep quiet! No matter what happens, stay put until I come for you. Don't move for any reason and don't make a sound."

"I've never seen that look on your face before. You're frightening me!"

His gaze was fixed on the horsemen. "Lie flat behind this tree and be still!" His voice was harsh, demanding. "Unless I'm wrong, they're two of the bastards who've been robbing trains. Those are money bags tied to their spare horses. They saw us, so keep your head down." Leo drew his revolver and stalked off, moving among the cottonwoods toward the riders.

*   *   *

Clyde jerked his horse to a halt. "That's him, Sloan, the sumbitch ridin' the train that day when Shorty an' Jim Bob got killed! I recognized him right off. He's the bastard who likely cut up Carl Pickins, too. I'd nearly bet money on it."

Sloan squinted in the sun's glare, remembering Carl and what had been done to him. "Carl was a friend of mine. Hold on to our spare horses while I kill this son of a bitch." He jerked his .44–.40 free of its holster and swung down from the saddle. "We got more'n ten thousand dollars in them bags, so don't let go of the reins for nothing."

"Be careful, Sloan. I hear LeMat's real good with a gun," Clyde warned. "Maybe he calls himself a picture painter, but he can damn sure shoot. Make sure the little bastard wearin' the sailor's cap ain't with him, either. He's a sneaky sumbitch an' he knows how to use a goose gun."

"I ain't no tinhorn, Clyde, so shut the hell up an' keep' an eye on our money. Killin' this bastard is gonna be real easy. I seen him wearin' them fancy duds just now. He looks like a goddamn drummer to me. An' you see how he's yellow as a chicken-killin' dog, runnin' behind them trees with the woman like he done."

Clyde had drawn his pistol, watching the cottonwoods where they'd last seen LeMat. "He don't appear to be all that brave, now that you mention it. I can't see him no more. He's hidin' from us, sure as snuff makes spit."

Sloan moved off the roadway to seek protection offered by rows of trees along the riverbank. He spoke to Clyde over his shoulder. "Whatever you do, don't let nothin' happen to them money sacks! You'll be the next man to die if'n you do—I'll see to it myself."

He rushed into the trees, listening, placing each boot on the ground softly, cautiously avoiding stepping on twigs or last year's leaves that would make noise and give his position away.

Pauline did her best to stifle an overwhelming urge to cry, covering her mouth with a trembling hand. The ominous look she'd seen on Leo's face left a chill in the middle of her chest and down her spine. The gentlemanly doctor she'd come to care for suddenly changed into a man she didn't recognize—his countenance, the flat expression on his face, mirrored in his eyes, sent fear into her hammering heart. She felt as though she scarcely knew him.

Leo shed his coat and tossed it on the rim of a cutbank at the river's edge. Water seeped into his boots where he crouched in the shallows, listening, waiting for a sound or a movement that would tell him where his adversaries lurked. One man had come down off his horse, slipping into the trees with a pistol in his hand while the other waited at the edge of the road holding their spare horses. Leo's first objective was to lessen the odds against him.

Moving quietly along the water's edge, making sure his boots made the softest possible sounds in damp river-bottom clay, he crept toward the highwayman guarding the money. It was a risk, leaving Pauline to fend for herself behind a cottonwood, but necessary. When the shooting started, Leo wanted her out of the line of fire. Keeping careful watch on the rim of the riverbank, bending down to avoid being seen, he moved closer to the spot where one man waited with the horses.

He heard a horse stamp a hoof, snorting through its muzzle. Leo raised his head above the sloping bank, aiming his pistol.

A bandit with a gun in his fist sat on a bay, his attention focused on the cottonwoods west of him, his back turned to Leo. Stealth, and the robber's carelessness, presented Leo with the right opportunity.

"Drop the gun," Leo said. "I'll kill you before you can turn around. Don't try me."

The cowboy twisted in the saddle, swinging his guns toward Leo, ignoring the warning.

Leo fired into the gunman's belly. The sharp report of his LeMat abruptly ended the silence along the Solomon River.

All four horses bolted away from the explosion. The rider atop the bay let out a yell as a stream of blood erupted from the front of his shirt. His horse lunged, rocking him back over the cantle of his saddle. He tossed his pistol in the air while he fell, clutching at his gut. The horses galloped away in four different directions before he landed on his shoulders and neck with a grunt.

Seconds after the gunman fell, Leo heard Pauline scream. His gamble that she would be safe behind the tree had backfired, for the shrill sound of her voice was proof enough that the second robber had found her hiding place.

Throwing all caution aside, Leo raced up the riverbank, breaking into a headlong run. More than a hundred yards away, he saw Pauline in the grasp of the other bandit, struggling to break free of his grip on her arm.

I'm too late, he thought, dashing among the trees, making a target of himself to draw the outlaw's attention away from the girl. *I shouldn't have left her alone . . .*

Sunlight glittered off a row of silver conchos around the crown of the man's hat. His pistol was aimed at Pauline's head.

Leo felt he had no choice but to try a desperate move. "The money!" Leo cried, running as hard as he could. "I'll take the money! You can have the woman!"

Leo was twenty yards away, closing fast, when the outlaw made a turn.

"Like hell you will!" he bellowed, bringing his revolver to bear on Leo.

A shot rang out, echoing through the trees. The hiss of speeding lead ended suddenly when the robber's bullet struck a cottonwood trunk. The gunman threw Pauline to the ground, bringing his pistol to bear on Leo, giving Leo the lone chance he'd been hoping for. Only ten yards separated the two men now. He had but one opportunity to kill his adversary without counting on careful aim and luck while he was running. Leo eased back the hammer and fired the LeMat's shotgun barrel at a range where he could not miss.

Grapeshot peppered the outlaw's face, tearing flesh from bone in a bloody spray of mangled tissue, ripping his gray hat from his head, puncturing his neck and upper chest with pellets. The force of impact lifted the gunman off his feet. He fell over on his back, screaming as the grass around him turned a deep scarlet hue, his pistol thudding to the ground beside him.

Pauline shrieked when she heard the explosion. As blood splattered her dress, she covered her face with her hands. Leo stood over the dying man, his muscles tensed with rage, until he was sure the robber would stay down.

Leo rammed the barrel of his revolver into the outlaw's mouth, although he was certain the man was dying. "Tell me who's behind the train robberies! If you don't give me a name, I swear I'll blow your goddamn skull apart."

Behind him, Pauline sobbed, horrified by what he was doing.

"Bell. Owen Bell," the robber mumbled around a mouthful of cold iron. "Please don't shoot me. I swear I'm tellin' the truth."

Leo pulled the pistol out of his mouth. "What's your name? And who's the man with you?"

"Clyde Wall. The other feller . . . is Sloan Wilson. If you ain't real careful, he'll kill you."

"He's already dead, Clyde. He drew his last breath a few minutes ago."

"Am I gonna die?"

"You're gonna die real slow."

"Jesus. I knowed I shoulda never got mixed up with Sloan. He got me killed, 'cause he double-crossed Tully an' wanted us to keep all the money . . . for ourselves."

"Greed has killed lots of men," Leo said. "You won't be the first, or the last." His killing urge was slowly ebbing now that the shooting was over.

Clyde's eyelids fluttered, then he slipped into unconsciousness. Leo glanced up at Pauline, and when he saw the look on her face, he knew things would never be the same between them.

"I'll round up their horses and tie them over their saddles," he told her. "We've got to take them back to town and tell Sheriff Jones we're returning the railroad's money. You'll serve as a witness to what this fellow said about Owen Bell being the man behind the Ghost Riders." His voice softened. "Sorry our picnic had to end this way."

Pauline said nothing to him, turning her back, walking toward the trees where they'd left the surrey. Leo felt a heaviness in his heart, yet he knew he'd been left with no choices today. He had done what he had to do.

Chapter 32

Leo drove the surrey into Abilene, leading the two gunmen's horses with their bodies draped across the saddles. It was a measure of the mood of the town that the gruesome cargo evinced only mildly curious stares from the townspeople. Leo was concerned about the way Pauline had been acting since the shooting. She'd been unusually quiet, sitting as far from him as she could on the surrey seat. Even though the shooting and its aftermath had been dangerous and bloody, he thought she'd shown more spirit than to let something like a little gunplay upset her so. Finally, he brushed away his misgivings. She'd either get over it, or she wouldn't. There was precious little he could do about it now.

Leo stopped at the Drover's Hotel and ran up the stairs to get Jacques. He was exhausted and needed someone to back his play in case any of the other Ghost Riders suddenly appeared.

When Jacques answered the door, Leo said simply, "Jacques, bring *Ange* and come with me. There may be trouble."

Jacques took in Leo's bloodstained clothes with a single glance. He grabbed his sawed-off shotgun and his hat from the corner and followed Leo down the steps, knowing he would be told the entire story when the time was right.

Jacques glanced at the dead men as he climbed in the surrey and sat next to Pauline, greeting her with a quick nod and a touch of his hat. Leo snapped the reins and guided the horses down the street, turning a corner and pulling the buggy to a stop in front of Dr. Sanders's house. As he walked to the front door and rang the bell, he hoped the two detectives were still there recovering from their wounds.

"Hello, Dr. LeMat," Mrs. Sanders said when she opened the door. "My husband still isn't back from the Calloways' place." She grinned. "I told him from the way Betty was carryin' she was going to have twins."

"Has Jack Ladd recovered from his wounds?" Leo asked.

She nodded. "If appetite is any indication, which my dear husband assures me it is, he's doing just fine. Would you like to see him?"

"Yes, please. Could you ask him to come out for a moment? I have some news for him."

Moments later, Ladd walked through the door, showing no ill effects from his earlier ordeal other than a slight limp and the bandages Leo had applied.

"Good afternoon, Dr. LeMat . . . ," Ladd began, stopping in mid-sentence when he spied the two dead men on horses behind the surrey.

He walked with Leo to the surrey and thumbed his bowler back on his head. "Well, what have we here?" he asked, turning his attention to Leo.

"These are two of the bandits who robbed the train last night," Leo explained. "If you'll look in one of those saddlebags," he said, pointing to Clyde's body, "you'll find the entire Ghost Rider outfit, his robe and hood."

Ladd stared at Leo. "And the money?"

"It's in the back of the surrey. I didn't bother to count it, or the gold and silver coins, but I assume it's all there."

"How did—?"

Leo held up a hand. "You don't need to know all the details. Because of my . . . rather tainted reputation, I'll let you and your partner take credit for ending these robberies. The one with the robe in his bags confessed before he died that the leader of the Riders is a man named Owen Bell. Pauline says he's a local rancher, and she can tell you how to get out to his spread."

"But what happened?"

"They rode up on us while we were having a picnic. I guess they wanted our lunch, however they found they'd bitten off more than they could chew before it was over."

Ladd shook his head. "Dr. LeMat, I don't feel right taking credit for what you did."

"Hell, Jack, you and your partner got pretty messed up trying to protect the railroad's money. It's only fair if you tell them you got the thieves who've been doing all the robbing around here."

Ladd took a moment to consider what Leo said, then stuck out his hand. "Thanks, Dr. LeMat. I'll spread the word to all the other operatives. If you ever need a favor of any kind, just ask any Pinkerton man. I'll guarantee you, you won't have to ask twice."

While Ladd and Leo were talking, Pauline stepped out of the surrey and began to walk slowly away.

Jacques jumped down and quickly caught up to her. "Pauline, *jeune fille*, what is wrong, young one? Why are you leaving?"

She turned to him with tears in her eyes. "Oh, Jacques. I don't know what to do. Leo, Dr. LeMat, he was like a different man out there."

Jacques nodded. He felt he knew what she

was about to say. He'd seen this reaction before from other women after one of Leo's killing rages. "Go on, *moi petite*."

"When those men appeared, Leo changed . . . his eyes . . . they became wild, and there was a terrible emptiness in them. It was as if he'd become like a crazed animal, wild with blood lust."

Jacques muttered, *"Un loup-garou."*

"What did you say?"

"It's a Cajun folk tale, about a creature called a werewolf, a large hairy beast. It seems, under certain circumstances, an otherwise ordinary man can be transformed into a monster, a vicious killer, one without mercy."

"Are you saying Leo has some disease?" Pauline asked.

Jacques wagged his head. "No, no *mon cher*, that isn't it at all! *Monsieur* Leo, more than most men, has his dark side. Fortunately, with him, it only surfaces under extreme . . . provocation."

"But he killed those men as casually as I would swat a fly," she said, a look of disgust on her face, "and he almost seemed to enjoy it."

Jacques understood how her gentle nature was shocked by what she'd seen. "Perhaps as casually as they would have killed you, had he not prevented it, *cher 'tite bete*."

She placed a hand on his arm, her expression

searching for understanding. "I *know* he saved my life, but that doesn't change the way I feel about him. I couldn't live with the fear of his terrible, dead eyes when he was killing those men." She drew herself up, wiping her tears away with the flick of her handkerchief. "Please give Dr. LeMat my regards, and my good-byes."

"As you wish, *mademoiselle*."

Hickok stood before his painting in Leo's room and grinned. "Damn, Doc, do I really look that mean?"

"You do, Marshal," Leo answered, as he poured the lawman another glass of wine.

"I believe you flatter me, Doc," he said, stepping in to get a closer look at the portrait. He fingered the wrinkles around his eyes. "Don't see these in the picture," he said with a note of sadness in his voice.

"Marshal Hickok, my aim is not to make an exact duplication of a subject," Leo said, handing him the wineglass. "For that, we have tintypes and Daguerreotypes. My object is to show the inner man, the soul of a person." He hoisted his own glass of brandy in a toast to the marshal.

"And you, Wild Bill, have the spirit of a Knight Templar, with the courage of a lion, and I hope that is what I have portrayed."

*   *   *

Jacques stood up from a chair in the corner of the room, "I'm sorry things didn't work out between you and Mademoiselle Pauline."

Leo shrugged, though his face couldn't hide his disappointment. *"C'est la vie, mon ami."*

"At least one of us, certainly the most deserving, has been lucky in love on this trip," he said with a smug expression.

Leo regarded him for a moment. "I've been meaning to ask you, my friend . . . how are you feeling?"

Jacques looked puzzled. "Fine, Leo. Why do you ask?"

Leo looked out the window to hide the slow smile forming on his lips. "No feelings of burning or itching of your private parts?"

Now Leo could detect a note of worry creeping into Jacques's voice. "What do you mean?"

"It is merely that I've talked to several men in town. It seems there is an outbreak of the Osage Pox, a condition carried by females of Indian descent in the area."

"What is this pox?" Jacques asked, his voice betraying concern.

Leo glanced back over his shoulder and noted Jacques was already beginning to scratch his crotch. "It is a disease transmitted by sexual relations. The male genitals become red and irritated. Suppuration sets in, and pus begins to form. Finally toward the end, the genitals rot off."

"Mon dieu!" Jacques exclaimed, clawing at his pants now. He rushed toward his bedroom. "I must find a mirror!"

Leo enjoyed a silent laugh. Herr Freud was right, he thought. The power of suggestion is amazing. Perhaps that would teach his friend not to gloat about his conquests in the future.